OTHER FINE GIFTS

Stories

Jeffrey N. Johnson

MEDDLER PRESS
Alexandria, Virginia

MEDDLER PRESS
Alexandria, Virginia 22308

ISBN: 978-0-692-94783-8

The author would like to thank the editors of the following publications in which many of these stories first appeared: Lost Among the Hedgerows - *The Sewanee Review (Andrew Lytle Fiction Prize)*; Fresh Eggs - *Night Train Magazine*; Legs of the Lame - *North Atlantic Review*; Tell You of My Dreaming - *Wisconsin Review*; Filling a Hole - *Potomac Review*; The Want of Molly - *Clackamas Literary Review*; Reappraising Jason - *South Dakota Review*; Modern Predators - *The Distillery*; Other Fine Gifts - *The Evansville Review*; The Waters of Casablanca - *Connecticut Review*; The Transfiguration of Mauricio - *Lake Effect*; Raw Toscana - *The Summerset Review*; Skating the Blumlisalp - *Aethlon: The Journal of Sport Literature*; With These Hands We Inter - *REAL: Regarding Arts and Letters*.

Printed in the United States of America

Acknowledgments

Gratitude to Heather, my first and last reader, and to Jim Johnson, as well as the poor-man's MFA program *Scrawl: The Writer's Asylum* and its various offshoots. Among my blessed reviewers were Diane Dees, Brenda Glasure, Dr. Emily Deans, Rusty Barnes, F. John Sharp, Tomi Shaw, Richard Martin, Sue Miller, Jodi Turchin, Harley Hill, Bob Church, Marian Wilson, Jeff Rose, Patsy Covington, Carolyn Steele Agosta, Terry Proffer, Lisa Dyer, and the late Lauren Ann Toca and Glenn Obsorn. It is often asked of writers if they have an ideal reader in mind, so I would be remiss if I did not mention the late Mike Sposito, gonzo journalist and Spinoza with a lightning bolt philosopher, now stationed at a legionary outpost, far far removed from the Grex.
Ecce Homo!

For Ava and Finn,
in hope they will one day tell their stories.

CONTENTS

OTHER FINE GIFTS

Stories

Lost Among the Hedgerows

THE ONLY CERTAINTY on the morning of our foreclosure was that I was going to paint a door. Not my own door, which was soon to be the property of a stranger, but a wooden frame glass door belonging to a contemporary-style house in the high-end hills above Lake Barcroft. I always start a job on the door most traveled, and I admit it's a calculated move. It's a play on sentimentality – the door as threshold to hearth and home, the place of greetings and goodbyes. I scrape and sand the plies of old paint, apply primer and two micro-coats of semi-gloss until the door is reborn. When I began my business, I noticed that homeowners' complaints about quality declined in relation to how beautiful their front doors looked after the first day of work. Those beautiful doors also toned down the grumbling over my rates.

The homeowner, Mrs. Romero, said over the phone not to knock at that hour, that the house was unlocked, so I grabbed my gear out of the van and tried not to think about what was happening on the courthouse steps. It was another muggy morning that had me sweating before I'd even started. I let loose with a four-inch scraper on the head trim, spitting sharp chips of red paint over my bare arms and shoes, and soon I fell into this zone I imagine a sculptor must feel when he works a piece of stone – a zenlike momentum as one hand scrapes and the other feels along, informing the first of angle, speed, and pressure.

I was halfway down the jamb when I saw him: the old man's face in the glass door. We held each other's eyes for a while, neither flinching. He could have been standing there watching me the whole time. His skin was dark and cracked like alligatored paint, and his face was bent out of shape, white hair mashed up on one side and the opposite cheek filled with weights. The long white robe he wore hung open, letting his sunken chest add to his other sunken features. I was looking at a life near the end of its curve.

He raised a shaking hand and pointed. I opened the door to introduce myself, but had to wait until he backed up his walker.

"Mr. Romero?" I said.

He ignored my outstretched hand and spoke from the side of his mouth, forcing the words. "There is no fright in you," he said, still pointing at my chest. "No fright."

It felt like I was being accused of something, but the accusation seemed like a good thing. I just stood there.

"Come . . . come," he said, wheeling around on the walker. I thought of taking him by the arm, but he didn't seem the type to want any help. We came into the kitchen and he took a seat at the breakfast table in front of a soggy bowl of corn flakes and a mess of newspapers. He was winded and sat there collecting himself, concentrating. Then he raised his good hand and put his thumb and index finger together as if pinching a word out of the air.

"I had ten thousand men under my command," he said, squinting for effect. "I see with my eyes. I had to know every one of them. You!" He slapped his hand on the table. "You're the one I'd have looked for. The way you came to the house. Your gait. And here, right here." This time he patted the table. "You would have risen quickly in the army." There was music playing in the next room, some faint classical piano, but nothing I recognized. The old man leaned over the paper and raised a magnifying glass, but he wasn't reading, just tracing aimlessly over the newsprint.

"I'll get back to work," I said. As I turned back down the hall, the front door opened and a woman I assumed was his wife came marching toward me – a military wife, the commandant of the house, and, judging by all the yellowed school photographs on the walls, mother of more kids than I could count.

"I asked you to go straight to work," she said, "not to bother the colonel."

"I was just introducing myself."

"Mr. Romero is recovering from a stroke and can't have any visitors."

She somehow got behind me, rushed me to the foyer, and shut the door right on my heel. That wasn't necessary, and I was about to go back and confront her when my cell rang. My wife.

"It sold," she said, as if not quite believing it would happen. Despite the early heat, my sweat went cold.

"We knew it would. We knew that."

"But you said it wasn't a certainty. That we still might have a chance."

I'd made an offer to the mortgage company the week before. Laid out payments we could realistically make and asked for a lower interest rate, not that adjustable rate time-bomb they sold us on. They never even countered the offer.

"I guess I was wrong."

"The new owner's attorney called already. He's giving us this weekend to get out."

I was getting angry. I didn't like the way Mrs. Romero rushed me out the door. Losing my house didn't help matters. I looked around the neighborhood, and it was all lush green, mature oaks and sycamores, well-tended yards, each house its own ideal. The surrounding hills sloped down to a private lake dotted with pontoon boats that never left their moorings. This was something I would never have.

"Did he say who bought it?" I asked. "The house."

"We've got until this weekend, Mick. This weekend."

∞

When I got home that evening, the letter was already there. A runner from Zietner, Anton and Kablast (from here on I'll call them Zak) slid it under the door. Wouldn't even knock. Nothing official, just letterhead explaining that the new owner would like to take possession of the house, and wouldn't my wife and I oblige by getting the fuck out before they have us evicted. Stapled to the back was a five-day Notice to Vacate.

"What's LLC?" Stacy asked as I read the letter.

"An investor looking to make a quick buck." I was hoping some young couple would have the winning bid. I could have stomached that better, maybe even handed them the keys myself. Then I could have called the whole purchase bad timing, taken my lumps, and started over. But an investor buying the house ticked me off. These were the same bastards who were running up the market five years ago, along with their lenders cooking the loan papers and hapless appraisers doling out equity like candy. Now that the market had tanked, the investors were back to clean up the scraps.

"I'm calling Mom," my wife said. "We're going back to Chapel Hill."

"Don't you think we should talk about that first?"

"We've got to rent a truck, get boxes, and packing tape." She was in panic mode, rushing from room to room. When she lost her job, she'd been like this. "We should have left weeks ago."

"There's plenty of time," I said, though I knew there wasn't.

"You're crazy!" She wheeled around to face me. "They're going to throw us out. The Sheriff's going to put all our stuff on the sidewalk, and the trash man's going to take it all to the dump."

"Most of what we have is ready for the dump. That old sofa your mother gave us. I doubt she wants to see that in her basement again." The sofa really was a mess. It looked like an upholstered loaf of bread that someone had sat on. The rest was crap from Ikea. We hadn't put anything into furniture.

"Then we'll take what we need." She rushed off to the bedroom where the suitcases were already open. "Mom won't like this, but neither will I."

Standing there inside the door holding Zak's letter didn't change the feeling that the house I was standing in was still mine. We were living in Dumfries, part of what the newspapers were calling the foreclosure "ring of fire" surrounding D.C. It was hastily built postwar housing that was now filled with as many immigrants as older natives. The streets were lined with a half-dozen generic house models with too many cars in the front yards and dogs barking at all hours through overgrown hedges and chain-link fences. Ours was a fifty-year-old split foyer and one of six foreclosures on our street. The other properties had been abandoned long before the banks took them over and seemed to have aged like homeless men – lawns overgrown, shingles missing, gutters fallen. A few had been broken into by roaming teenagers and vandalized in obvious ways. By comparison our house was a model home. It was the first Stacey or I owned, and I had literally touched every square inch of the place – spruced it up with crown molding and painted every room, got down on my hands and knees to stain the hardwoods, installed new toilets and vanities. Stacy picked out the appliances and countertops, the stuff that sells a house, the stuff that makes a home.

Stacy was banging things around in back, cursing and slamming drawers. It was hard to listen to and made me feel bad for her, after all she'd been through. I walked back to the bedroom where she was sitting on the floor stacking photo albums and scrapbooks in a box.

"Sugar," I said. "I'm not going anywhere."

∞

Painting is the perfect job for thinking, since painting requires no thinking. It's a tactile pursuit, something for the body's rhythm and flow, freeing the mind to wander, plan, and plot. When my thoughts are tapped out I can simply follow the scraper or brush with all the concentration of a shrub. After putting the final coat on the Romero's front door, I began working on a windowless stretch where I knew I could be alone with my thoughts. Forsythia was growing wild against the house, so the first thing I did was cut it back to give myself room to work. The only window was at the far end of the wall, and as I hacked my way there I noticed the Colonel watching me. I didn't lock onto him this time, just kept cutting back the hedge. He never left his post and watched my progress like he was keeping watch over his men. After I dumped the last armload of brush in the yard, he rapped on the glass and awkwardly cranked open the casement window.

"Watch for those damn booby traps," he said. "Could be anywhere." I needlessly looked around my feet, knowing he was kidding. He was talking badly, always with one hand to help animate his words, but he was in his right mind. "This first lieutenant, good friend, MacCabe, red haired, a new baby stateside . . . he commandeered a farm house to billet his men for the night. Took the biggest bedroom. There was this painting on the wall hanging there crooked. Nice painting . . . French countryside. He straightened it and boom! Blew him in half. The charge was in the wall at waist height," he said, leveling his hand. "Killed two boys on the wall's other side too. Heinies liked to trap bottles of liquor and cartons of cigarettes. We knew about those, but the picture was a new booby trap. When they brought MacCabe out of that house twice, then we knew about crooked pictures."

I was mesmerized by this guy. He made my problems seem trivial. No one was dying of foreclosures.

"The letters I had to write," he said. "Parents, wives." He looked like he was about to break down. The Colonel had commanded ten thousand men and here he was crying in front of a stranger. I wasn't sure if it was noble or pathetic, but he was somehow putting me in a place of acceptance of what I was going through.

Beyond the shadows in the glass I saw Mrs. Romero come to the door. She stared at me, but said to him, "Come on Colonel, it's time for your exercises." He nodded and turned his walker, but a thought must have come to him. He looked over his shoulder.

"The last thing MacCabe saw was that painting of France. All he had to do was look out the window."

∞

Sunday afternoon Stacey's brothers were moving our things into a rental truck to haul back to her mother's house in Chapel Hill. We spent the first six months of our marriage there, and it's not something I planned on repeating. Her brothers said they'd be back for my sorry ass in a few weeks. Just watch. We drank beers on the couch Stacey's mother said not to bring back. I was right about that.

"At this point it's more a matter of principle," I said.

"It's a matter of being a stubborn ass," one brother said, as the other stared at the wall where the television used to sit.

"They can't legally turn off the utilities, and they can't force me to pay rent. Besides I need a place to stay until I finish this painting contract. So let them evict me."

Stacey came in dragging her suitcases. "You boys having too much fun, or can you possibly get me the hell out of here?" The brothers abandoned their bottles and carried Stacey's bags to the truck. They still had the airline tags on the handles from our honeymoon in Aruba. We hadn't been able to afford a decent vacation since.

"I just talked to an agency," she said, staring around the room as if finally realizing this was the end of five fruitless years. "I got temp work as soon as I want."

"Take some time off," I said.

"Mom won't have that for long. Not while I'm under her roof." She crossed one leg behind the other and balanced there, looked ready to fall, then turned to face me. "Are you planning on joining me?"

I shouldn't have hesitated, but I didn't know how to explain it. "I've got some things to take care of. And I've got a job to finish."

"Fine then."

"I've got commitments to keep."

"Do you?" she shot back. "Do you remember *all* of your commitments?"

The look in her eyes scared me. It wasn't the beautiful face of the woman I had married, but was the anguished face of someone who had lost everything. I knew then that she feared for our marriage. I had let her down and I didn't know right then what to do about that. "I'll be down soon," I said, trying to calm her.

"How soon?"

"The first thing we'll do is get a place. I promise. No offense to your mom."

She sniffled. "She doesn't want us there anyway."

It seemed we weren't wanted anywhere. Stacy kissed me quick on the lips, as if it were a duty, and rushed out to meet her brothers at the U-haul where they were shuttering the back door and staring at the dark clouds approaching from the west.

There was no television or stereo. I had an old laptop, but no internet access. I was left alone to wander the empty rooms, hands in pockets, scuffing the floors and leaning on door jambs, everything made foreign by the lack of furniture and the absence of my wife. I opened the door to what we had misnamed "the baby's room." All that was there was a mattress on the floor where our visiting friends crashed. Stacey had been picking out colors and drapes for two years, but about the time we realized we needed help and started looking at fertility clinics and all the costs, she lost her job. Then we got stuck with COBRA payments, and within another six months the interest rates were adjusted upward. We stopped picking out baby names.

There had been no rain for a month, but the hot streak was finally breaking with a late afternoon thunderstorm. I went to the window and watched it come on, first in big drops, then the wind and finally the deluge. The gutter over the window overflowed and soon the water came down in a sheet like another pane of glass. I could feel the weight of all that water pressing on the house, the roof sagging, the rafters splitting, pipes bursting, the entire foundation beneath me sinking into the earth.

Across the room I noticed a nail sticking out of the wall. It was a four-penny brad and I wiggled it out of the gypsum, taking a flake of paint with it. Then I went around the house with an old bucket of spackle and pulled all the old nails and patched the damage. It was a silly thing to do, but painting was the one thing I knew best and could still take pride in. Something inside me wanted the house to look immaculate when they threw me out. As I made my rounds and touched up the plaster, I thought of poor MacCabe and how he didn't know what was waiting for him inside that wall. And it occurred to me that all I did was cosmetics. It's what you can't see that kills you.

∞

Zak stopped by early Monday morning, looking not at all surprised to see me. He was an overconfidant punk right out of law school who should have had a price tag hanging off his sleeve. He craned his neck to see inside and said matter-of-factly that the owner was starting the eviction process immediately. Court dates were running about two weeks. "I was right about this one," he said, handing me his business card, which I flipped into the yard.

I carried the tub of spackle from the night before back to my van and stood there scanning its dark interior. My toolbox was open and crap was spilling everywhere, tools and material I didn't even remember buying: a torque wrench I never used, a spool of copper wire from God knows what. I grabbed a sanding block and picked out a few cans of interior latex in the right colors and finished the touch-up work on all the nail holes. The wet paint didn't quite match, but I knew it would be fine once it dried. Then I went to a window and raised the sash. I knew every window in the house just like I knew the floors and the walls. The last owner had hired a lousy contractor who painted them all shut, and I had to use a utility knife to slice through the gobs of paint in the corners to free the sashes. I had scraped and repainted every one of them. Now I was going to do it right. I took a one-inch brush and spread the latex thick inside the double hung tracks. I did the same to the top sash and closed them with a rag ready to catch any overflow. It was a beautiful job. The corners were visibly clear, and after a few hours, no one, even a skilled painter with a utility knife, would ever open that window again.

∞

It was late morning by the time I got to the job, and Mrs. Romero wasn't happy about it. She ran a tight household, and that made me consider how I do business. All my competitors made a mint hiring illegal immigrants at slave wages to do all the work, but the quality wasn't there. I wasn't going to have one of those businesses. I like working with my hands, not running between multiple jobs yelling at people in broken Spanish. The fees are about the same, but doing it myself takes more time. Quality always takes more time.

"I was lost three days in the Cotentin," Colonel Romero said through the window I was working on. "Hedgerows my ass. Swamp! I was wet for three days. Three days!"

I had gotten used to the Colonel watching me through the windows, and I wondered if it wasn't me that brought out his memories, as if he were looking at himself over a half century ago. I imagine one day I'll look back and digest all I did right and wrong, but I hope I'm not consumed by it.

"They dropped us all over hell," he continued. "Had to use the stars to guide me at night. Imagine a whole army scattered over two hundred square miles. But it confused the Germans more than it did us."

Mrs. Romero had given up trying to separate us, and it seemed I'd even earned her approval. Once she brought us both iced tea, and as she left she needlessly told me the colonel was a war hero. That was the role of his life. As she strode back to her chores, he said aloud to no one, "She is the hero."

∞

After I finished painting the Romeros' back windows that afternoon, I went home and finished painting my own, or at least the ones that used to belong to me. Thinking back to Colonel Romero's stories of crooked pictures and Bouncing Betties, it occurred to me that only the retreating army left booby traps, and here I was in full retreat with the enemy on my heels. The sealed windows seemed trivial. I was basically leaving them the same way I bought them five years ago. I needed to do more, and I had only a handful of nights.

The vandals down the street were rank amateurs. They'd kicked holes in the walls and broke a few banisters. I worked more subtly. The house had cast-iron plumbing, not copper, and it was already rusting in spots as it traveled along the basement ceiling. From inside each access panel behind the bathrooms I reached in as far as I could with a v-shaped file and made wedges in the supply pipes. Then I finally found a use for that spool of copper wire rolling around my van. I wound the wire around the gouged pipe and tied it off, then ripped up one of my old T-shirts and wrapped a soaking strip of fabric around the wire and sealed it all together with duct tape. Give it a few years, I thought. But that was a delayed fuse. I wanted something more immediate.

I went back to the van and found a half case of expandable foam insulation. I grabbed a can and squirted just a bit into an electric outlet. It hissed and oozed out in a sticky yellow ball. I shot less into the next slot and kept the overflow to a minimum. It was quick work and I was getting unusually giddy running from room to room, dropping to my knees and giving the can of foam the slightest pulse. At this point I couldn't help myself. I grabbed a pipe-wrench and dropped the P trap from one of the vanities, then let loose with a can of foam deep into the wall. It never bled out, must have expanded up and down the waste pipe. Even so I took another can and sprayed in most of it before it finally pushed back at me. I got the P trap on quick and sat there tingling on the floor by the toilet. I'd replaced that toilet too. This wasn't so hard. Shut off the cold water, drain the tank, only two bolts to deal with. I filled the four inch waste pipe with three cans of foam that must have bubbled halfway to the roof.

∞

I had come full circle and was painting the last window on Colonel Romero's house. Over those weeks I gained his wife's trust, and now she allowed the colonel to sit outside and supervise my work, but he said nothing of my technique or abilities, no heavy critiques or little niggling comments that I was accustomed to from homeowners. I was free to paint and he was free to reminisce. He kept my mind off the next day's eviction, of which the sheriff had informed me earlier that week.

"We were on a scouting mission. Heard some rustling in front of us," the colonel said. "I told my men to get down and cover me. I went ahead, came into an opening. This German soldier, a boy, he comes out of nowhere, running; carries his rifle like he could barely lift it. Just a boy. He was as surprised to see me as I was to see him. We just stood there staring at each other. Just staring. Then my men riddled him, shot him to pieces. He never took his eyes off mine. I'll never forget the look on his face. He was so surprised. To this day I still see that boy's face. I'll never forget it."

For a moment, I thought I saw the boy's face too and saw the horror that was forever frozen in the colonel's memory. His own surprises likely diminished as soon as he moved his family to this neighborhood. Like many people living by the lake, the Romeros probably spent their leisure playing cribbage and sipping gin on one of the pontoon boats permanently anchored to the shore. All those years residing in Eden, yet he still couldn't erase that boy's face. All he could talk about was the war. It had made him, and I wondered if the foreclosure was making or unmaking me.

∞

The rain and lightning were coming on every evening, leaving the dusk grey and the ground steaming. After it passed I stood in the gathering darkness and listened to the drips of water off the trees and gutters, heard the distant traffic and watched lightning bugs light upward and disappear. I remembered seeing a documentary about how if left to nature most of man's creations would disappear in a mere hundred years. Wood-frame housing was one of the quickest to go. Once the shingles curled up and water made its way inside, it was easy.

I grabbed my electric drill and a quarter-inch bit and climbed through the hatch into the attic. It must have been a hundred degrees up there. I laid on the subfloor and got used to the dim light washing up through the scuttle. The roof was sheathed with half-inch boards that seemed harder than what the lumber companies sell today. I placed the drill bit between two rafters and squeezed the trigger, really pressed into it. The shavings fell onto my face, so I shifted and pressed harder until it pushed through and hit something spongy. I adjusted the pressure and let the bit do its job until it went through the shingle. Twisted curls of black tar came out with the bit. I rested there and trained my eye on the hole until I saw a quarter-inch circle of moonlight seeping through. A second later a drop of water landed on my nose.

From memory I drilled Orion through the roof, followed by the Big Dipper, Leo and a few other astrological standards. Then I riddled the Milky Way across the back slope as my forearms ached, covering myself with shavings of wood and tar. Two hours later I was exhausted, soaked from hot sweat and ice cold drops of rain, which made it bearable. For a minute I thought I might die there and laughed at what the authorities would think of finding me like that. But I wasn't ready to die.

∞

I would like to have slept late on the last morning in my house, but these things happen early. I had been sleeping on the mattress in the baby's room since Stacy left, and I could barely climb out of it from the soreness from the night before. Everything I had was already in the van, so I made a paper cup of instant coffee from the hot water faucet and waited.

A knock sounded on the front door at 9:00 A.M. sharp – three timed blows by a hard fist. As I crossed the room I noticed that the house was beautiful, immaculate even, but for the old sofa against the wall. I opened the door and smiled at the grim-faced sheriff. Zak was standing behind him smiling back as he reared his head to peek inside. "Good morning, Sheriff," I said, raising my cup. I felt pretty good.

"Morning Mr. Hadley. I have a writ of possession signed August 28th, 2010 by the Honorable Judge _____ of the Prince William County General District Court, Commonwealth of Virginia . . ."

He was reading off a script, though he shouldn't have needed to. He probably did a dozen of these a week. My mind glossed over at all the legalese and I just stared down at the threshold separating our shoes, his fine polished leather and my paint-splattered canvas. It felt like he was reading a canned eulogy for a homeless man no one knew or cared about. Zak would have been the undertaker, smiling in the back row so long as state dollars were paying for the funeral.

When the sheriff was finished and asked if I had any questions, I said no. "Here you go, Zak," I said, feeling lighter as I handed him the keys. Zak stared at me funny.

A small band of Latinos in matching baby-blue T-shirts was loitering near a white box truck that was way too big for what they were going to get out of that house. And it hit me right then that I thought of it now as *that house*, not *my house*. I stepped over the threshold.

The AC wasn't working in the van, so I cranked down the window. Hot, humid. There were more storms in the forecast. I didn't look back at the house, but my eye caught the scene in the rear view mirror. Zak was chatting it up with the sheriff, and two of the movers were carrying the sofa to the sidewalk. They dropped it there and stood staring at it while one lit a cigarette. Then I noticed something parked on the street that didn't belong there, a Mercedes SUV with tinted glass. That's when the lightness of the morning passed and my spirit began to crash. I knew then the war was lost. I couldn't see the victors' faces, just the reflection of the trees in the blackness of the glass. They were waiting for me to leave.

As I drove away, the full weight of what had happened and what I had done was on me, and I realized it was something I would always carry. I would have risen quickly, the colonel had said. Maybe another time and place, but not now. My rise was going to be a slow moaning hell, and only after a full retreat and more humiliations. But I like to think my rise began the moment I took the southbound ramp onto I-95 to make a new home with my wife. I had failed her, and I had failed myself without her. I missed her face more than I could believe, and, rounding that long blind curve out of town, I was afraid of the distance that separated us. My accounts were empty, credit cards maxed, and mind scattered over the miles. I had never felt more alone, but I wasn't alone. There was an army of us.

Fresh Eggs

EVERY SATURDAY MORNING James and his ten-year-old son went to buy eggs. They climbed into an old Ford pickup, set the choke, and after some protest the truck fired up. James slapped Nathan on the knee and off they went with the windows cranked down and a cool windstorm flailing their hair. The truck slowed through town, past the Baptist church, the supermarket, and the antique shops. James pointed to the old boarded five-and-dime where he worked as a young man, and Nathan nodded. Some Saturdays, Nathan would point to the five-and-dime first, and his father would nod.

"Dad, why don't we buy eggs at the supermarket like everybody else?"

James pondered the question as they rumbled over the loose boards at the railroad crossing. A grain elevator with a faded Southern States logo sat to one side like a giant, abandoned milk carton.

"These eggs are fresh, Nathan."

They put the town behind them as the road ran deep into the Piedmont, down two-lane roads so narrow the side mirror clipped the leaves of passing trees. James glanced at his son. The boy's eyes were closed and his chin rested on an arm over the window sill, letting the morning air splash over his face. James knew the road by heart and thought he could have closed his eyes too.

A few miles out of town they coasted into a small valley of fresh-cut ochre fields. A lone farm house sat in its belly surrounded by ridges of ancient cedar. Though it was still early Fall, smoke rose from the chimney. Planted around its perimeter were a number of outbuildings: barns, sheds, and coops, at one time painted bright red but now sanded down by time and weather. A mass of honeysuckle was pulling down the fence where they hit the potted driveway. The sound of crushing gravel signaled a shift that they were entering a world of old ways and hard attitudes.

Lewis Pitman looked as though he had been waiting for them, but had likely been sitting on his back porch all morning. He gripped the arms of his rocker and stood as tall and straight as he could. Resting one hand on his walker, he raised a Mason jar of goats milk to his lips. As he drank, the tracheostomy tube in the center of his throat surfaced like a plastic button sewn to an old hide.

James climbed from the cab and brushed his mussed hair to one side. He welcomed the smell of the fresh cut hay. Nathan hopped down and mingled with the company of roosters bobbing in the yard.

"Lewis, you're looking good today," James said, though not without concern.

Lewis Pitman responded with a large exhalation, a half whisper – the other half whistling through the tube in his throat. A garbled 'thank you' came out. Though strained and bleary, his voice retained a memory of the powerful man he had once been. He set the Mason jar aside and extended his hand.

"Growing like a weed," the old man warbled, motioning to the boy. "Remember you . . . that age." He kept gripping James's hand for balance, then grabbed the walker with both hands and rapped it once on the floor. "Come," he said. Lewis pushed ahead, resisting James's attempt to help him off the porch. The two men took a painstaking pace across the yard with Lewis and his walker leading by a half step. James kept near with a ready hand. They passed the wire cages and the warped chicken coop, and came to a barn with an open face to the south. Inside the cavernous space sat Lewis's tractor, a rusted hulk of a machine, its tubes and tires dry-rotting and the engine pasted with oily chaff. Scattered to one side was a host of implements: a disk, several plows, a rake and baler, all being consumed by a jumble of pokeweed.

Lewis paused to catch his breath, then nodded toward the old machine.

"What you figure it's worth?"

James considered the obsolete tractor.

"Hard to say, Lewis." James rubbed the day old growth on his cheek. He feigned interest, taking a closer look at the engine "You found a buyer?"

Lewis shook his head as Nathan came up from behind.

"What's that for?" Nathan asked, pointing at one of the boxier attachments.

Lewis shook a finger at the contraption, then deferred to James.

"That's a baler," the boy's father said.

"Your daddy. He knows," Lewis said. Nathan turned to his father, whose face seemed older in the shade of the barn.

"Years ago I used everything here," James said, motioning all around. "Mr. Pitman used to hire me every season." Lewis stood a little taller. Nathan climbed on the baler and surveyed the ruins.

"Like around my age?" the boy asked.

"A little older, but not much," his father said. "It was a long time ago." He couldn't bring himself to look at Lewis, whose eyes were fixed on an arbitrary spot in the back of the barn. Lewis's sons were not farmers and had gone off long ago to find their own ways. Before leaving for college, James's days on the Pitman farm were hard working and happy. He had never since had a job where he could feel accomplishment in his muscles and joints. He lamented that his son might never know such rewards. James planted a foot on the front wheel of the tractor, staring at the ground as he spoke. "Lewis, why are you trying to sell this old stuff?"

Lewis sank a little into his walker. "Damn taxes," he said, the spirit wheezing out of him. "Can't keep up."

Nathan climbed onto the tractor and bounced into the saddle. "Does it still work?"

Lewis raised a weak hand and twisted it in the air. The key was in the ignition and James told his son to turn it. The boy stared back reluctantly. "You're old enough now," his dad said. "Push in the clutch. Stand up on it if you have to. Slip it out of gear. That's right. Now push the button." He pointed to the fat metal knob in front of the stick that looked like it could have fired a torpedo. Nathan pushed it hard. The tractor groaned three times and fell silent.

"Battery," Lewis said, shaking his head as though it was always the battery.

A crushing sound came from behind the house as a shiny flatbed truck roared into view and spit gravel down Lewis's driveway. A big brown arm stuck out the driver's window and waved, less in hello than in announcement of his arrival. Nathan waved back, but his father just watched.

The truck made its way to the large hay barn toward the rear of the property. Two workers jumped out the far side as the truck backed to the double-door. Their clothes were dirty and wrinkled at every joint, and might have held their shape if taken off. In unison the men yelled, "Whoa!" and the truck jerked to a stop.

"Lewis," James said with some weight, "I see you're still renting your fields to Millen. If you don't mind me asking, how much are you charging him to cut and store?"

Lewis stood firm. "Going rate."

The going rate in what year? James wondered. He had sworn to himself to keep his nose in his own business, but he knew Millen too well. "You best be taking fifty percent of his gross and not a penny less. Plus storage, mind you."

The man with the big brown arm jumped from the cab and walked toward them with a smile, lips parted but teeth locked together. His khakis were pressed and in his golf shirt pocket was the outline of a cell phone. He left deep footprints in the grass.

"Damn Lewis," Millen said, barreling toward them. "I've been working myself to death. I'll be seeing my grave long before you see yours."

"A good day . . . that will be."

"James," Millen said, staring right into his eyes. "Your boy?"

"Yes, you could say he belongs to me. How are you, Millen?"

"Work and more work and I still can't make ends meet."

"You're doing well enough for that new flatbed."

"Three words, my friend. Tax *de*-duction. Your tax break is sitting there on that tractor. I drive mine." He took a step closer to Lewis and looked down on him. "We're keeping the last two hundred bales here 'til New Years."

Lewis raised his head as best he could. "Best pay . . . this time," he said with an exasperated whistle.

"Put it on my tab," Millen said, walking away. "You know things are tight."

The three of them watched Millen march back to the hay barn yelling orders at his workers, who were already throwing bales out of the loft onto the flatbed.

James planted his hands on his hips. "He's not paying you in a timely manner?"

Lewis turned and motioned again toward the tractor. James shook his head and stepped back into the shade of the barn where a bush hog was languishing in the next stall. He took a closer look and pondered it for a moment. He sighed quietly to himself. "Lewis, we might be able to come to a price on this."

"Dad, we already got a lawn mower."

James winced as he glanced at his son. He thought of his five acre lot and then blocked out what his wife would say. "We don't have a bush hog or a tractor big enough to pull one. How about it, Lewis?"

"You decide," Lewis said. "Next week."

It was plain that Lewis was wearing down, so the three of them walked back to the house. James helped the old man onto the porch and into his rocker as Mabel popped open the screen door to greet them. She seemed as wide as she was tall, and the porch creaked loudly as she stepped on it. She held out her cupped hands.

"Got chick feed for you, Natty." She poured the tiny pellets into Nathan's hands until they overflowed. He trotted back to the chicken coop, sprinkled the feed on the dirt floor, and watched the birds peck and bicker.

"What do you say?" James called to his son, whose thank you sounded back across the yard.

"Is he going to be a farmer?" Mabel asked hopefully.

"Can't say." He watched his son and at the same time took in the whole farm, noting how much had changed over the decades. He was sad that Nathan would likely remember this place only as a childhood novelty, a petting zoo at best. But perhaps the boy was better off not having such deep roots. He turned back to Mabel. "Lewis tells me your tax assessment is up again." The old man made no sound but for the soft creak of the rocker. His wife regarded him nervously and wiped her hands on her apron.

"Don't rightly know how our land is worth what they say it's worth," she said.

"Have you applied for relief? They got programs to – "

Lewis thumped his walker on the porch. "I've always paid my share!" he cried out, and then lurched forward with his chin up to catch his breath as the air wheezed through his neck. James rushed to his side, though he didn't know what to do.

"He's fine, James," Mabel said, resigned to fate, yet not without feeling. "Lewis don't take no charity."

James took Mabel's arm and guided her to the far side of the porch.

"How far is Millen in arrears?"

She knotted her hands in the apron, and didn't seem able to untangle them.

"He said he's gonna work out a payment plan."

"How bad is it, Mabel?" She was about to break down. James felt bad for pushing.

"We ain't seen nothing since spring. And that was only half what he owed us from last year."

Nathan came back to the porch with fresh grass stains on his knees. James watched the men at the hay barn and caught their banter, cursing, and lewd jokes as they loaded the flatbed.

"I'll talk to him this week," James said.

"No, James. Don't."

"Mabel, I'll talk to him. He needs talking to."

Her damp face eased, but still showed lines of worry. "Let me get your eggs," she said, finally untangling her hands. She reemerged a minute later with a grey carton and handed it to Nathan. James felt the coins in his pocket, then pulled out his billfold.

"I don't have exact change today," he said. "Ya'll just take two dollars." Mabel appeared grateful, then embarrassed as Lewis grabbed his walker and rapped it on the floor. She hurried inside and came back fingering a rose-colored change purse. She scraped out a few coins, but James waved her off.

"You can make change next week. I don't need an IOU." He turned to speak to Lewis. "You can feel right about charging a little more for such fine eggs." The old man didn't flinch as he gazed across his dormant fields.

Mabel hollered thank you as James and Nathan climbed into the truck. Nathan held the carton of eggs in his lap like a present as his father started the engine.

James called out the window, "Lewis, if you can talk your hens into laying me two dozen for next week, I'd be obliged." Lewis tapped his skeletal hand several times on the arm of the rocker. "And I'll look into pricing that bush hog."

The driveway circled the house and passed the cloud of hay dust drawing from the barn where Millen was still barking orders at his men. Young Nathan raised an eager hand and waved, but Millen turned away to answer a call on his cell phone. The boy looked at his father and saw that his face was tense, his jaw tightened. As they hit the pavement, Nathan flipped open the carton and ran a finger over the perfect little brown domes.

"Dad, the eggs at the grocery store are only a dollar-forty a dozen. That's only fifteen cents more than what the Pitmans charge, but you paid them two whole dollars."

James was silent as the road climbed to higher ground. His hands squeezed the wheel, and his eyes fixed on the rear-view mirror as they rose above the valley.

"We don't come here for the eggs."

Legs of the Lame

AFTER THE DEATH OF HIS FATHER, Randy decided to become Randall and began saying things like "glory" and "praise God" with alarming regularity. According to the folded pamphlet he carried in his pocket, this was the first step to a new life. His wife, Jackie, smiled passively at one of these biblical intrusions at her parents' supper table one Sunday afternoon. Her father and mother exchanged glances and chewed their food longer than necessary. Jackie's little brother, Sean, only ten years old and therefore having accumulated the least sin in the family, was the only one innocent enough to laugh out loud.

"So *Randall*," Jackie's father said, with a bloody piece of meat hanging from his fork. "I suppose God had something to do with the stock market tanking on Friday?"

"I suppose He did," his son-in-law answered, repressing a sudden flare of his old temper. Right before his father dropped dead, Randall looked a little like Jesus, but he'd recently shaved his beard and cut his hair to a more modern Christian appearance. Now he looked more like an undertaker with his hair cropped to the scalp and white shirt buttoned to his Adam's apple. He swallowed a mouthful of potato salad, and added, "Perhaps the market would recover if we made a habit of saying grace before supper."

Jackie chimed in quick and asked if she could refill anyone's tea. Carl Huss chewed his meat and looked to his wife, Cheryl, who sat at the head of the table with a polite hand in her lap. Her presence seemed to calm him. Sean sat across from his father and giggled as he pushed peas around his plate. Huss shook his head and sighed, picked up his steak knife.

"If saying grace made a difference, I'm sure Wall Street would have been onto it by now."

Jackie looked relieved that her father had held his temper. She filled the glasses tall with tea, then took her husband's hand. "Daddy," she said, staring at his sweep of greying hair. "We wanted to ask you." For their first anniversary they planned a weekend trip to Williamsburg, and they offered to take Sean along. He hadn't even traveled out of the county except for a class field trip to Luray Caverns, she explained. He needed to start seeing the world to better understand things. It had been Randall's suggestion.

"They got rides there?" Sean said excitedly.

"That's Busch Gardens," Jackie replied. "We're going to Williamsburg. That's like where all the colonies started and everything." Randall nodded, yes, that's what they wanted to do. Sean picked at his food, less enthusiastic since rides were not part of the deal. Jackie glanced back and forth between father and mother. Cheryl Huss smiled in approval as her husband wiped gravy off his plate with a tuft of bread.

"Well go on," he said. "I ain't got time to take off."

Several days each week Randall stopped on his way home from work to seek counsel of the Reverend Cavender. Having yielded to depression and drink after his father's funeral, it was Cavender who raised Randall from the depths. He was captivated at the way the reverend would call him by his proper name and not just holler "you" or "boy" in his general direction. For the first time in Randall's life someone was taking him seriously, and he owed the reverend his attention in return.

The Glen Hollow Baptist Church sat a mile out of town and was capped by a charred steeple that had been struck by lightning five years prior. Cavender had the money to replace the steeple, but refused to do so. His parishioners gossiped that he wanted the scar on his temple to remind everyone of either the soul's incontestable blemishes, or the simple wrath of God – either would do.

One afternoon they were walking between the church and the old pine forest. The late autumn grass was deep green, and a small patch of moss-covered headstones sprouted from it on one side of the churchyard. Cavender wore a brown corduroy coat with fake white fur circling the hood like a frosted wreath. His bloodshot nose supported thick black glasses that magnified his gaze. Randall always wanted to face him, to be under those eyes he knew could see him for who he really was.

"Your father was a God-fearing man, was he not?" Cavender's lips barely moved as he spoke.

"Yes sir," Randall replied.

"Then he may be on the grandest of journeys. And do you know what I believe?" Randall kept a half step ahead, leaning forward to see the man's face. "I believe he is *on* that journey," the reverend declared. Relieved at this positive revelation, Randall relaxed his pace and stared into the grass as Cavender continued.

"Now he had his flaws, but flaws are mans' nature. He has been forgiven, has he not?"

Randall rubbed the scar on the back of his hand and nodded.

"So now it's time for *you* to ask for forgiveness. You must take up the cross daily. I'm talkin' obedience." After some deep thought, timed as if he were speaking from the pulpit, Cavender added, "Do you want to be accepted by your father?"

Randall's eyes lit up in hope that it was not too late. "Yes, Reverend." He slipped his hands in his pockets and opened and closed his fists.

Cavender turned to face him. *"Go ye into all the world and preach the gospel to every creature."* Randall, it is your duty and privilege to make disciples. Tell your friend, tell your neighbor, tell the next person you meet. Tell them the good news."

∞

Randall and Sean had been distant but accepting of one another as new brothers-in-law, but Randall thought they might become something more. He had recently been stopping by his in-laws' to throw the football with Sean in the back yard, something he missed in his own childhood. Though Randall's body carried many scars, none were from football or other games played in youth. He was certain, with enough time spent, that he could become an important figure in Sean's eyes. He fantasized that he might even become a hero to the boy.

Williamsburg was confined to a weekend round-trip in Randall's VW Beetle that suffered from a lack of heat and insufficient upholstery. Sean was scrunched in the back seat, though it didn't appear to affect his spirits. He and his sister told jokes the entire trip, while Randall forced a grin and clutched the wheel with both hands.

Randall guided Sean through the colonial streets from shop to shop, from shoemaker to blacksmith, and touched him awkwardly on the shoulder and head, always trying too hard to explain things. Whenever he drew a blank, which happened often, he told Sean that this was a different way of life, and summed it up with a "praise God." In one of the gift shops he bought Sean a coffee mug with a horse drawn carriage on the side. He also bought him a little flag to put on his desk. The display held hundreds of different flags, and Sean chose one with a serpent that said, "Don't Tread on Me." He asked what it meant and Randall said "tread" must have something to do with the snake's slippery skin. Sean looked doubtful, but he wanted the flag anyway because he was interested in snakes – just last summer he found one in his back yard and chopped its head off with a hoe.

On the way home Sunday evening, Randall took the highway exit into town. Jackie said, "You forgot, we got to take Sean home."

"You look tired. I'll drop you off first. Besides," he said, perking up, "I have a surprise for Sean."

Jackie gave him a suspicious look, but said okay. They pulled in front of their apartment and she climbed from the car with Sean tumbling out behind her. She held her hands together and blew into them. "You take him right on home. He's got school tomorrow." Randall didn't respond, but just sat there staring. Sean gave his big sister a hug, then moved to the front seat and popped the wafer-thin door shut. He held the mug and flag in his lap as his brother-in-law drove them out of town on a two-lane road. Sean looked between his feet and could see the pavement rushing by through a hole rusted in the floorboard. They had joked about it on the way to Williamsburg, but now it grew in size and gave him a chill.

A mile shy of his in-law's house, Randall turned the twittering Beetle onto a gravel road. The left headlight jiggled, making a strobe effect, and the gravel struck the bottom of the car like corn popping. He pulled into a field access where the fence notched in and a wide aluminum gate blocked the way.

"What are we doing here?" Sean asked.

"I told you, I got a surprise," Randall said as he cut the engine. He pulled a duffel from the back seat, then removed a single black volume like it was a delicate relic he had stolen from a museum. Countless yellow stickies curled out of the last half of the pages. He got a flashlight from under the seat, and the red glow of the coning lit their breath and flushed their faces.

"Your mother and father have never taken you to church, have they?"

Sean thrust his hands in his pockets and shivered. His hair was mussed from the long day of travel and his nose was running. He whispered no, as if uncertain of his answer.

"We're going to take care of that," he said, opening the book. "You at least know who Jesus is, don't you?"

"I know 'bout him."

"You know you got to love him? That you got to believe in him?"

"I guess."

"What I'm talking about is . . . is a different way of life. Look, look here." Randall's finger shook down the page until he found his verse. "*He that believeth and is baptized shall be saved; but he that believeth not shall be damned.*"

Sean squeezed his legs together and leaned closer to the door.

"Look, Sean. You're of age to decide. You got to confess that you're a sinner. It ain't no private matter."

"How do you know I'm a sinner?"

"Look. Don't get defensive. Don't act like you're on trial. This ain't no trial. This is like . . . like a child asking his father for forgiveness."

"What did I do wrong?"

Randall grabbed Sean's hand from its warm pocket and slapped it on the bible, held it there with his cold pressed hand.

"Listen to me, boy. Jesus died on the cross for your sins. You got to believe. Do you want to go to hell? Tell me you believe."

Sean stared blankly into dash. "Okay. I believe."

"Don't just say it. You got to mean it. Stop that – keep your hand on the book. Do you accept Jesus as your own personal savior?"

"I don't know."

"You got to know. Stop fidgeting. Don't you know Jesus died for you?"

He tried to pull away and began to tear up.

"I don't know nothing 'bout that," he cried.

"Come'on now, boy," Randall said, squeezing Sean's hand. "Look. My daddy's dead now . . . dead and gone, and I'm okay with that. Do you know why? Do you?" The child was frozen. "Cause I'm gonna see him again, for sure I will, just as surely as they nailed Jesus onto a couple old boards. We both got the faith. Now how would you feel if your daddy was dead, right here this second? Dead and buried and returned to the maggoty earth where he come from."

"I don't know." Drops of water trailed around his nose.

"Then you got to believe in salvation." Randall droned on as the boy stared into the floorboard and sobbed. He finally settled down and agreed with everything he was told, swore his faith on the book and said archaic phrases he had never said before. When Randall was satisfied he put the worn volume back in the duffel and started the engine. His fingers opened and closed around the steering wheel like little star-bursts.

"You're now on a great journey, Sean. You're justified. Praise God."

When they pulled up to Sean's house, the silhouette of his mother wrapped in her shawl stood waiting in the doorway. He jumped out of the car and ran into her open arms.

"A glorious evening, Mrs. Huss," Randall hollered to her.

"We'll talk about your trip next weekend," she said smiling. "We want to hear all about it." As the VW buzzed into the night, she placed a hand on Sean's head. "What do we have here? What treasures did you manage to find?" Sean wiped his nose with his sleeve and showed her the coffee mug with the little carriage on it that said "Williamsburg." Then he felt his pockets. The flag was gone.

∞

"You ain't got no business talking God with my son." Carl Huss had led Randall into his back yard, as his wife didn't want anything in the house broken.

"I ain't got business. I got a moral duty."

"You want to preach, find a parish. You want to guide a kid on some pious path, make one of your own. I made Sean and I'll bring him up my way."

"Being that you don't see fit to rear your own children in the church, I thought I'd take it upon myself to do God's work."

"You're one sorry-ass representative of the Almighty. Wasn't but a few years ago you were terrorizing this town. Drinking, vandalizing, knocking up who knows who." Huss stared Randall into the ground. "Don't think I didn't know."

Randall felt trapped, caught in the vice of this past he no longer claimed. "I've chosen a different way of life," he said indignantly.

Carl paused and took a long breath. "You will not talk to Sean about this again. Do you understand?"

"I understand," Randall said, but he never agreed. He understood the difficulty faced by the believers, the suspicion cast by the nonbelievers, the persecution endured by the disciples.

As Huss walked away shaking his head, Randall heard him mutter, "moron." A pallor washed over him and dampened his mood for the rest of the evening. As he drove home he searched for passages in his head to comfort him, but by the time he opened his front door he had only grown angrier, throwing his coat on the floor and screaming at Jackie for his dinner. He clicked the tv remote in circles for an hour before flinging the control across the room where it shattered to pieces. In the early hours of morning, long after Jackie had gone to bed, Randall sat naked on the bathroom floor with his head between his knees. The book sat open on the cold tile as he tore through the pages in seek of solace. The next day was no better as he went to work delivering packages and letters from place to place on ridiculous deadlines. Near the end of the day, he dumped the last two boxes on his route into a dumpster behind a 7-Eleven, then sought the help of Reverend Cavender.

Cavender adjusted his glasses and shook his head. He warned Randall of men like Carl Huss, and to subvert their efforts to kill faith and God and ghost. "A pox on the church, men like Huss," he said. Randall drew the validation he was looking for and now understood that his father-in-law was the enemy. He told Cavender about the boy.

"I baptized you and I baptized your daddy," Cavender said, his eyes staring through Randall. "Now a savin' is a good thing, but a savin's only as good as the man's faith behind it. Them's just words borrowed from God, but less than filth in a man's mouth, as man ain't nothing but a chimp. What you done, Randall, is a non-savin.' Now a baptism, that's far closer to a written guaranty – a first class ticket, at that. Faith follows close behind a good immersion."

The common baptism shared with his father warmed Randall and drew him closer again to this lost figure, despite the lingering memories of the beatings. His legs had been the best defense as he learned to curl up in a way where his thighs could take the worst blows. Later on he used them for running as he was faster than his liquored father. But on days when the old man's reflexes weren't compromised, he would strip Randall to his underwear and turn him outside for an hour in the cold. "That'll teach the boy," his father had said, buckling his belt.

After many years of abuse and belittlement Randall finally told his father to fuck off and drop dead, and he did, just two days later as he stopped to light a cigarette on his way to the mailbox. Only a month from retirement, Randall's father had resigned himself to the hobby of lawn care to occupy his golden years, and he was probably pondering what kind of grass seed he would spread in the spring. He landed face down in a big puddle on the pavement. The coroner swabbed a little mud from his mouth and nostrils, but none was inhaled. He was dead before he hit the earth.

"With a father like Huss," Cavender proclaimed, "that boy won't have no guaranty, warranty, or what-hither if he don't get baptized. Everything opposed to the light is darkness. You may yet pry the boy from his heathen."

Randall nodded and stared blankly into the little patch of mossy tombstones.

∞

Two weeks later Sean stayed after school one day and missed the last bus home. His mother called Randall and asked if he could pick him up. The late autumn days grew short and by the time Randall got to the school the sun had waned and a cold darkness hardened the land. Sean was laughing and joking with another stranded classmate, but the smile dropped from his face as Randall pulled to the curb, waving his righteous hand. Sean pushed through the front door of the middle school with his coat open, slid into the Bug, and said "hey." The slamming door sounded like the click of a suitcase latch. Randall probed him, asked how his day was, but the boy's humor had dried up and he only answered in okays and grunts. He saw his snake flag on the floorboard and read the words. When he looked up, he turned forward and back.

"This ain't the way home," Sean said.

"We're going on a little trip. It's a surprise."

Sean zipped up his coat. "I'm gonna be late for supper."

"I told your mom. She's fine with it."

The boy stared at a small clapboard church as they whizzed past. A lone spotlight caught the partially burned steeple, making the whole structure look off-kilter like a false prayer. Then he grabbed the dash as Randall took a hard left onto a narrow dirt road delving into the pines behind the church. The bug bottomed out in the ruts like a boat scraping the sand bars.

"I wanna know where we're going." Sean's voice wavered with the car.

"I said I gotta surprise."

In a quarter mile the field of view opened wide and dropped off as if an infinite space lay before them. They came to a steep incline where Randall brought the bug to a rest on an old concrete boat launch. He killed the buzz of the engine, but let the headlights pierce straight ahead where they split the darkness in half and lit a narrow band of rapids. Nearly in line with the old road, the white water was all that remained of an old ford. The roar of water over rocks, normally a sound of meditation, only isolated them in the frozen wilderness.

"Do you trust me, Sean?" he asked, reaching for his duffel.

"My daddy said we can't talk no more 'bout those things."

"Your daddy's a sinner and he's going to hell," Randall said, as if speaking an indisputable fact.

"He's not."

"Do you trust me?"

"He's not a sinner." Sean turned away.

Randall grabbed his book, got out of the car, and told Sean to come on. He tromped toward the river, then stopped and turned as the headlights lit his grey slacks like glowing steel bollards. He came to the passenger side and tried the latch.

"Unlock the door," he said. Sean reached over and locked the driver side too. "I said open the damn door."

"No," Sean shouted.

"You have to trust me, boy."

Randall slipped the bible into his coat pocket and dug into his pants for the keys. No trust indeed, he grumbled. The boy just don't understand. He turned the cylinder, popped the door, and took Sean by the arm. "Come on," he said. "You'll thank me for this." Sean pulled back and kicked, but Randall got him by the neck, heaved him outside, and bent his skinny arm behind his back. The little flag fell to the ground.

He led the struggling boy to the river where the rapids grew louder. Sean screamed as his feet hit the water. Randall was too exhilarated to feel the ice cold water fill his shoes or even rise to his crotch as he pushed through the current into the middle of the river by the large rocks. He heaved the boy onto a flat slab of dry stone, then pulled the bible from his breast pocket and sat it at his feet. "On this rock I shall build my church," he said, grinning widely. Sean made a shivering ball of himself and shrank away from his brother-in-law. Feeling the effects of the cold, Randall climbed onto the stone and lay on his back.

"Sean," he said, winded and wide-eyed. "This here . . . this is where I was baptized. And my daddy was baptized." He sat up and pondered the river, saw it divided by the beam of light. "You got just two directions. Upstream or down. Fight the current or flow with God." His eyes grew accustomed to the dark and fixed on the starlit sky.

"I'm disappointed in you, Sean. You lying about your faith the other week." Randall thought of Huss's interference and disparagement, his rejection. Then of Cavender's eyes. "But you're about to experience a burial and resurrection. All is about to be forgiven."

As Randall rose, he felt a sharp blow and his vision splintered. The rock hit him above the right ear. The boy's shadow jumped past him and splashed away. He crouched there and wavered for a moment, as if being held up by strings attached to the stars, then fell downstream with a splash. He bobbed up and down before finding footing where the white water flattened into smooth ribbons.

"Booooy," he yelled, but his voice was drowned by the wrath of the rapids. Blood and water ran down his face as he pressed a hand to the wound on his head. His words came long and slow. "Run . . . you moron." He struggled against the current toward the rock of his father's church, but his legs were shaking too hard to move. The band of glistening light over the water was unreachable and only deepened the blackness that surrounded him. "No good," he said, now realizing he was alone. "Just like your father." In his daze and despair he turned away from the light and thought for a moment he saw his own ghost, an apparition of a frightened boy scrambling down the road in the red glow of a car's taillights.

Tell You of My Dreaming

EVERYONE SAID IT WAS TOO SOON, that I should take a week off and do whatever it is grieving people do, but I was too young at the time to know what those things were. I was sixteen and needed to make miles. The faster I confronted the next random tragedy, the faster I might grow out of the shock and back into life's equilibrium. So on a Monday morning in March, the day after burying my father, I rose defiantly and went back to school.

As I climbed aboard the bus, my usually boisterous classmates fell silent. I had never been the center of attention before, but I was suddenly surrounded by a commotion of veiled whispers and glancing eyes. The bus driver gave me a pitiful look in the rearview mirror as Becky Ratcliffe boarded and sat by my side. It was rumored she had a crush on me, though I had none on her. She had a plain freckled face and always hid her flat chest by hugging her books. She released an impish 'hi' and seemed afraid to touch me. We rode on in silence until the apparent strain was too great. She blurted out, "It's not the end of the world," then wrapped a strand of hair into her mouth and didn't say another word the rest of the trip. Though I knew she was right, she looked as appalled at what she had said as I was at hearing it. At that point I wanted to run, to sprint over the clover fields and into the pines and remember how to breathe, but I just sat there in a cool fog, casting my mind out the window into the changing landscape.

My family lived on a few acres in the Virginia Piedmont along the rural fringe of Washington, D.C., back when it was just a government town. Our neighbors were either transplanted bureaucrats drawing federal paychecks or farmers who could proudly trace their lineage to one of Mosby's Rangers. But our community makeup was changing by the day as the land passing before me was threatened with prosperity. Developers were nibbling outward from the city, spawning their generic housing and making millionaires of our last generation of farmers just as they were readying for the nursing homes. My father spent his whole life among these bucolic hills, and had he come back from the grave ten years later, he would not have recognized the country.

My best friend, Dennis, was a trusted distraction. During the mourning period imposed by my mother, he kept me informed of all the parties I was missing, which to a teenager is another kind of loss. News of who had the latest kegger, who threw up, and who almost got laid only reminded me that I was cut off from the world, as did the silent evenings spent working jigsaw puzzles and watching *The Love Boat* with my mother. Dennis's great love was a Dodge Challenger 426 he'd rebuilt with his dad. With its twin scoop hood and primer coat the color of coffee grounds, it was as important to him as any girl in his life. He sometimes raced on weekends at Old Dominion Speedway, but he'd been caught stealing rubbers from his father – by his mother – and he wasn't racing anytime soon. He'd been grounded in the middle of my social exile, and he called me all restless one Sunday night.

"Jake, you and me gotta get out. It's been two weeks of this nonsense and I'm itching," he said. "And you. You gotta be wasting by now."

I agreed. I was wasting, but not in any way he could understand. "Aren't you still grounded?" I asked.

"Another week, but I don't give a shit. I'll sneak out."

"You don't have the keys."

"You think I didn't make a copy?"

The following Saturday I worked up my nerve and told my mother I wanted to go out. She sat in a tightly stuffed chair with her legs tucked under and her pale fingers holding a *Southern Living* magazine. She wore all polyester, a plain blue blouse, dark pants, and no makeup. Her black hair stretched tight over her scalp and looked thinner than usual, but she likely hadn't washed it recently. She had been letting herself go. A black and white movie glowed from the television, something with a young Jimmy Stewart, but she didn't appear to be watching. The hand that held the magazine went limp.

"I don't think you're ready to be going out just yet," she said in a measured voice.

"I think I am."

"You're still waking up screaming."

"That doesn't have anything to do with anything," I said, though I wasn't sure if this was true.

She tilted her head and stared absently at the TV. "I just don't think you need any excitement right now."

I told her I was bored and kicked my foot in that sulking way that works for only a teenager. "I need to get out of the house."

She gazed at the program as if Mr. Stewart might be able to talk to me, set me straight. Then she raised her magazine back to her face. "I want you home by midnight."

Her easy capitulation surprised me. Of my parents, she was the disciplinarian, and I expected no longer a leash in my father's absence. She was also the stronger one, or so I had thought. I had never before seen her cry, but she was crying often now and I didn't know what to do about that. She cried every night. She cried alone in her bedroom and wouldn't answer when I knocked, but I guess I had some restless nights too. Occasionally, in the late hours when the evening was darkest, she would come to my room to see if I was okay. Backlit from the hall light in her long robe, she would stand in the doorway and watch over me like some weary-worn sentinel. I always told her everything was fine – I wanted to show her how well I was handling things. After she'd leave I would open the window by the bed and fill my lungs with cool air and wonder if the next day would be any better.

"I'll be back before then," I said, feeling guilty for abandoning her.

I went upstairs to shave, despite the less than impressive growth. Not long before, my father had taught me how to use a razor, how to feel the grain and endure that first fiery shock of aftershave. Once a week was more than enough, but after his passing I began the ritual lathering each day as if I had earned some right-of-passage.

I walked the quarter mile to Dennis's house down a two-lane road that humped over the hills like an endless black ribbon unfurled over the land. Light patches of fog from an earlier thunderstorm obscured the way and the pavement was still wet, on which oncoming headlights made a nebulous blur and sprayed a cool mist as they passed. When I reached Dennis's house I waited behind the garage where his Dodge sat to one side. Almost ten o'clock and the house was dark. A downspout still dripped from the storm and the tree tops blew above me, denser now, with the tips of new leaves filling the April sky. Spring had dropped a scattering of shriveled magnolia blossoms all over the car, and I began picking them off the windshield. After a few minutes the back door inched open and Dennis slipped out of it. He held up a single key on a ring, and even in the blackness I could sense the smile on his face. We clenched our teeth as we pushed the car down the gravel driveway, and as it rolled onto the pavement we jumped in and drifted into the fog. When he felt we were clear, he slipped the car into gear and popped the clutch – the Challenger lurched and roared, and we sped off. In his excitement he gave a little yelp. He tossed a plastic baggie from his jacket into my lap and pushed in the cigarette lighter.

"Just one for now," he said. He popped a cassette into the dash and Blondie's "Dreaming" beat through the car like a racing pulse. Then he looked at me for a second like he didn't know me, like I might be a cop or something. The lighter popped and I lit one of the joints from the baggie. The windows were down and the damp breeze felt good. I leaned back and exhaled slowly, watching the smoke whirl into the night. I passed the joint to Dennis and he did the same. After a couple of hits, he wound down a notch. "So how's your mother?" he asked.

"About the same."

"It's about time you got out again," Dennis said, scolding. "You got to get on with your life."

"I suppose so."

"We need to get you stoned and laid, is what we need to do."

"I suppose."

Gatti's Pizza, or at least the parking lot, was where everyone went when nothing was going on. All the cars were washed out in the same colorless pallor from the sodium lights, and the place made me feel color-blind or cast in a bad sci-fi movie. Even peoples' faces were pale and less attractive, and all this did was remind me of what the undertaker had done to my father.

Our friend Kurt was already there in his Ford Bronco, and he had two girls in the front seat we didn't recognize. One was rougher than Kurt as wild threads sprouted from her jean jacket and tangled with an electrified wad of hair. A cigarette hung from her lips like she was about to hurl an insult. Her friend seemed more grounded. She was thin and pretty in her pink and white button-up sweater. She looked like one of those magnolia blossoms before it fell on Dennis's Challenger. I had to wonder if the two girls were friends or whether Kurt had picked them up from different sides of town. Kurt sat there grinning, sporting a ponytail that might have been cut off an old mare. His camouflage jacket had numerous pockets for contraband, and he always looked like one hand was wandering whenever a girl was nearby. His older brother, who was nineteen, supplied him with beer, and that made Kurt a popular guy, though I knew when each of us came of legal drinking age his popularity would plummet.

We pulled alongside them, and Kurt tossed us two cans of Stroh's still attached to the plastic lacing. They flew in Dennis's window, and when he tried to catch them he dropped the burning joint between his legs.

"God damn you," he said.

Kurt cracked up and beat his dash with one hand. "Beer is beer," he said. "You should be grateful for what you have."

Dennis got things under control. He handed me one of the lukewarm cans, then drew his attention to the girls and caressed his steering wheel.

"I'm Dennis. What's y'all's names?"

"This here's Tina and that's Joanne," Kurt said for them. "They go to Woodson."

Kurt always tried to hook up with girls from the neighboring high school, which wasn't surprising given his reputation at our own school. Tina lowered her cigarette and said 'hey,' then examined Kurt's dash like she had just found something stuck to the bottom of her shoe. Joanne sat erect and waved, looking on with some trepidation as if something dangerous might be lurking nearby.

Tina lost interest in the dash and eyed me. "What's wrong with him?" she asked.

"That's Jake," said Kurt. "His father died last month, but don't hold it against him."

"That sucks." She blew a long dramatic funnel of smoke as if saying, "what the hell, we're all going to die someday." Joanne gave me a smile tempered with pity. It was a smile I'd seen a lot of in school.

Kurt wanted to take the girls four-wheeling, so we made for what had been the country, but was being transformed into Burke Centre, a 1,700 acre construction site, one of dozens of new housing projects grinding up all the land in the county. A three-quarter moon cut through the breaking clouds as Kurt led the way in his Bronco to the newest tract, and Dennis and I followed. We dimmed the headlights to parking lights as we turned onto a heavy gravel construction road and wound into a small valley where all the trees had been cut and piled in a kind of woodland holocaust. In the darkness the silhouettes of bulldozers and backhoes might have been destroyed tanks and artillery left scattered across a battle plain. All mud and muck and destruction. I knew my father had known one of the old farmers who had sold out there, and I scanned the killing fields, wondering where their farmhouse might have stood.

We approached a small construction trailer with a security light burning on the opposite side and parked in its shadow. Kurt jumped out and locked the front wheels. Dennis held his beer in one hand and the baggie of joints in the other. "Boy, girl!" he called, hopping in front next to Tina. I slid in by Joanne as she crawled into the back seat. Kurt gunned the engine and felt the transmission – made sure the wheels were properly locked – then gave his version of a rebel yell and ran the truck straight into a broad puddle at the bottom of the valley. The girls screamed, Dennis hollered, and I held on as we splashed into the soup and fish-tailed to the other side, tires spinning. Kurt roared up the hill and whipped around, sending mud in a spiral before plummeting back into the mess. Joanne grabbed my arm.

"Okay, okay," she said when we reached the other side. "Let me out."

"Aw, c'mon," Kurt protested. "We ain't even got stuck yet."

She jumped out of the cab. "That was cool and all, but it's something I can mark off my list of things to do in life. You guys go ahead." The truck dripped and the engine hissed. The stirred-up mud smelled of something dead and rotten.

"I'll stay too," I said. This wasn't what I had in mind for my first night out, and I felt out of sorts. We began walking back toward Dennis's Challenger.

"Y'all stay cozy," Kurt hollered. "And you watch out for him, Joanne. He ain't kissed anyone since he made out with his father."

I honestly didn't know what to do with that. Part of me wanted to drag Kurt out of the truck and beat him to death, but I just crawled into the driver's seat of the Challenger and stared at the "No Trespassing" sign stapled to the construction trailer. I heard Dennis tell Kurt to shut the fuck up just as he revved the engine and spun away, sending another rotting plume of muck behind them. Joanne sat in the passenger seat and wrapped her arms around her, not in a protective way, but in a kind of stretch that she shook off like she was shedding an uncomfortable moment.

"What did that mean?" she asked.

"Nothing," I said.

Then without hesitation, she asked how my father died. Others had inquired, but no one had been so forthcoming. I was slow to respond.

"Heart attack," I said. "He just dropped to the kitchen floor. That was it."

"Were you there?"

"He was only forty-six."

"So you were there. When he died?"

"Yeah."

She looked straight ahead into the same sign, its mean and blocky letters lit only by the breaking moonlight. "I can't imagine my father dying," she said, as if reading the words. "I don't know what I'd do if that happened." She turned to me. "What did you do? I mean, when it happened."

"He kept a bottle of nitro pills in the medicine cabinet. I knew he had some problems. So I go to get his nitro pills. Mom said no. She got the pills. She told me to do CPR. I got certified last year in health class, so she wanted me to do CPR." I felt my breath getting short and I wanted air, but I just sat there. "So I got my hand under him, under his neck. His mouth just flopped open."

"Was he still alive?"

"I felt for a pulse. Gave him compressions."

I didn't have much else to offer. I just stared at that sign.

"You gave him mouth-to-mouth?"

I didn't say anything more and she was quiet now, as if I'd given her enough to digest. My mind was on that morning. He had taken the day off and hadn't shaved. I could still see the specks of white phlegm wedged in the corners of his mouth and taste the Tums and Old Spice. I felt the oil from his nose between my fingertips and his one-hundred grit sandpaper face on my lips. I wasn't supposed to be thinking about those things anymore.

I don't remember how much time passed before Joanne spoke. "Look," she said, pointing. "See that big wall of dirt? That's the dam. We're below the water line for the new lake." It seemed to give her a sudden lift to be in a place where no one would ever be again. Maybe she thought I would feel the same.

"How do you know so much?" I asked.

"My parents have a contract on a house here." She gazed around aimlessly, as if looking for a face in a crowded stadium. "Somewhere. It's supposed to be finished next fall." We no longer heard the whining of Kurt's Bronco, but in the distance laughter and cursing sounded near one of the other trailers. Joanne said, "In six months we'll be under water."

"So we'll drown."

"No. We'll swim." She tugged my sleeve. "It will be much better than this."

I don't remember whether it was a calculated maneuver or a hormonal reflex, or for that matter who even moved first, but we drifted into each other and kissed. For a time, though I held her and held her tight, I forgot about the rest of her body. I wanted her mouth. I wanted to melt into it, to sink into her lips, and I lingered on her face in a trance until I was about ready to pass out. It was really something. Just smooth and wet and warm, and of course I had kissed girls before, a few, but not like this. Then fearing she might get mad if I didn't try, I laid a hand on her breast, but she pulled away.

"One step at a time," she said.

Glass shattered from somewhere across the construction site and there was more cursing. Hot damn and holy shit. But Joanne and I kept doing what we were doing – getting lost in it. I didn't care what the others were getting into, and I don't think she did either.

As several more crashes echoed over the field, a flashlight singed our faces through the fogged windshield, and I sprung away from Joanne as if her body were suddenly electrified. A hand tapped on the glass and made a circular motion. I cranked open the window, and the man behind the light said, "I'll need some identification please." I dug for my wallet and scanned the field as if I could send the guys a signal. "Don't worry about them," the officer said. At that moment three flashlights came on and bobbed across the far end of the site centering on the other trailer. The outline of the Bronco sat to one side. When the cop finished examining my driver's license, he said, "Young lady, I'll need yours as well."

Joanne sat with her hands folded and knees together like she was sitting in a church pew, though she looked uncertain, as if doubting the essence of the homily. "I don't have a driver's license yet," she said.

The officer groaned and shined the flashlight around the cab and on the floor-boards. "Being as you two still have your clothes on, why don't y'all just go on home." He stared across the field. A light glowed from the open door of the trailer, and you could see the outline of a man being handcuffed. "We got bigger fish to fry."

He held the flashlight away from us, and in the ambient light I glanced at the ignition. No key.

"Sir," I said. "It's not my car. It belongs to one of them." I pointed weakly.

"Well then, God dammit. I suppose y'all will have to come in too." He looked us up and down as we climbed out of the car. He shook his head. "No use in cuffing the two of you."

By now four squad cars sat at the construction entrance with their lights sending red dance-floor flickers across the battlefield. We could see the three vandals being led across the site with flashlights at their feet, and each was directed to a separate car. Joanne and I were wedged into the same back seat as Tina, who was cuffed and pissed, smelling like Marlboro Lights and rancid mud.

Right before we pulled away, I saw my friends in the other cruisers, each sitting awkwardly with their arms cinched behind them. Kurt seemed to be mocking the whole situation, and why not? He'd gotten out of them before. But Dennis sat ill, bent over, and crying hysterically. Then I remembered the pot. I did not see Dennis again until the following school year.

We'd lost track of time – it was past one o'clock when we arrived at the police station. After everyone was interviewed, they slapped me and Joanne with misdemeanor trespass. One officer said we were lucky. It was no worse than jaywalking or a parking ticket. The contractor had been called and he wanted the vandals, who were now in the back of the jail in iron cells. It would take more than a few signatures to get them out.

Joanne and I waited together on oak chairs to one side of the squad room. I stuffed my ticket in my pocket, but she studied hers. She slouched in her chair like a little air had leaked out of her. I told her I was sorry. She asked what for.

"Everything," I said. "What do you think your parents are going to do?"

"Kill me." She shrugged, then tightened those lips I knew so well. "It's not the end of the world."

My mother arrived at the station at one-thirty in the morning wearing her heavy wool coat, and I thought that in her panic she must have thrown on the first thing within reach. Her hair was mussed, looking thinner than before, and each eye was circled with a rash of tired skin. She glanced at me only long enough to acknowledge that I was indeed alive, then she sat by a grey metal desk where a fat cop was scraping mud from his shoes with a screwdriver. The officer handed her a clipboard, and she signed the piece of paper that was on it. They talked for several minutes and the officer eyed me, then gave my mother a sympathetic nod. In my shame and embarrassment, I went to her only when she motioned for me to do so. As I walked away, I didn't look back to Joanne. I didn't even say goodbye.

After a silent car ride home we sat at the kitchen breakfast table and I told her the story – at least most of it. I surprised myself when I told her about making out with Joanne and about how different it was than kissing any of the other girls. She listened and made no motion. She didn't nod or scold or shake her head – I don't think she even blinked. When I finished my story she pushed herself up from the table, went to the refrigerator, and poured herself a glass of milk.

"Your daddy and I got caught once," she said, leaning against the counter. She swirled the milk in its glass and stared into the whirlpool. "When we were dating, not long after he got back from Korea, we parked by the Jefferson Memorial. I don't know what got into us," she said, her eyes fixated in the milky white. "We were naked when that policeman found us. I don't know what made us think no one would see us." I couldn't think of anything to say. These were the lives of my parents I didn't know, and it wasn't my mother speaking anymore. It was like watching a very personal interview with an actress, one whom I'd known only from a single typecast role.

"You know," she said, "he used to wake up screaming too, only he dreamed he was still in battle."

"How'd he get past it?" I asked.

"I'd hold him. Tell him he was in a better place." Maybe it was the hour of the morning or the lack of sleep, or knowing the sun would soon rise, but my mother stood there wistfully, dwelling somewhere else for an isolated moment, leaving me alone in the room. "But it sure was pretty," she said, coming back. "Being there like that, and that monument all lit up." She finished her milk and set the glass in the sink. As she passed to go to bed, she put a hand on my head.

"Turn out the lights when you go up."

That night, after recounting the evening, I slept all the way to morning in as deep a sleep as I'd had in a long time. I thought too that I had dreamed again, this time of something soft, but I can't say I remember it. My mother never cried again after that weekend, at least not that I know of. Maybe she had cried herself out. Maybe a month worth was all she had in her.

I never saw Joanne again. Later that week, after Kurt's release from juvenile hall, I asked him for her number, but he claimed not to have it – he didn't even know her last name – then he razzed me for making out with a fifteen-year-old. 'Jail-bait Jake,' he called me, but soon, after I turned eighteen, we did not call each other anything.

Today, nearly thirty years later, when I go to visit my mother I sometimes pass through Burke Centre and wonder if Joanne's parents still live there. And I wonder what steps she took to get past that evening, past that minor crisis of parental scolding as well as the accumulation of all the other joys and tragedies that have piled up behind her, each marking distance in a life like dashed stripes on an aimless highway. One time I tried to pick out the body of water where beneath the surface Joanne and I had lingered and touched lips, but I couldn't find it. The old wounded landscape has healed beyond recognition, transformed into a world my father would not recognize, a neighborhood reborn and well worn; the trees mature, the lakes full.

Filling a Hole

TINNIE PAYNE SAT on his only surviving kitchen chair, a mission style relic, whittling a piece of maple into a stone-lined hole in the ground where his house once stood. His spotted hands worked the knife unconsciously, shucking little curls of wood toward the stone chimney ruin on the other side of the hole.

With the help of a cane, he rose and squinted down the hill. A pickup truck cast a plume of dust as it pulled onto the property. He felt the pockets of his overalls for his watch, fingering nails, pieces of wire, and other oddments ready for unexpected jobs that might require such things.

The truck bounced up the hill, shaking its driver like a pea in a can, and came to rest by Tinnie's weed-smothered sidewalk. Tinnie thumped his cane on the ground with one hand and waved his pocketknife up and down in the other.

"I tell you to go slow, an' I tell you, an' I tell you. God dammit. That's why it's so rutted, is you gunnin' your damn truck up it like a loose bull."

"Sorry, Mr. Payne," the young driver said. "I'll slow it down next time."

"You'll slow it down or you'll stay off it. I'm too old to be digging up my driveway. You're late. Get on up around here. Wood's waiting for you."

Tinnie guided the truck with hollers and hands waving, around the old house foundation and up the hill to where leaning trees looked over the ridge.

"Back her up, now. Back her up," he called, using his cane to guide. "Whoa! I said, whoa, God dammit!"

With a rip of the emergency brake the driver jumped out of the cab and pulled on his gloves.

"Only got time for a half cord today, Mr. Payne. I'll be back next week for the other half."

"Now maybe I just won't be here next week. Maybe I got other things I got to get done."

"You're here every day," the young man said, heaving the first split piece of oak into the bed with a hollow metal clang. The wood was well seasoned, split and abandoned on the ridge three years before.

"I'm here every day of my own choosing, but I don't give no guarantees I'll be here the next time. You won't be getting no wood with my gate locked up, now will you?"

"Well, I guess not. I'll tell you what. You tell me when you'll be here and I'll accommodate you."

Tinnie was ready to argue, but pondered the man's concession. He removed his hat and thought hard, scratching behind his ear as though he had found a small lump of clay.

"A week from today. I'll be here a week from today."

"Great, so will I."

"Now hold on, I didn't say what time. You said you'd accommodate me." After a pause, Tinnie decreed, "Noon. You be here at noon, and I'm not waiting next time."

"That'll be fine."

The man began chucking firewood into the truck bed like spent artillery shells. Tinnie supervised for a time, then pivoted on his cane and turned his sunken eyes to the bulk of his estate. Beyond he could see the entire valley being slowly consumed. Houses mushroomed on the south end where his neighbor's cattle once grazed. To the east the forest had been clear-cut for timber and replaced by bands of asphalt awaiting driveways. The west was still virgin and worried.

He pried open his tin and plucked a wad for his cheek. That'll be fine indeed, Tinnie thought. If he were my son, I'd a raised him better. He don't understand none at all. He just don't get the things that's got to get done. Got fence that needs mending. Get that fence mended and I can get down to the auction. Black Angus'll look good out there next winter. Gotta shovel out the barn stalls; get them ready. That loading ramp is looking to need work too.

Tinnie reviewed his checklist twice as the truck filled behind him. The hollow foundation in the center of his property was like a black hole sucking in his ideas. The young man topped off his truck, then handed Tinnie a sweat tipped check for the wood.

"You sure have a nice spread here, Mr. Payne. If you ever think of selling part of it, I'd be interested."

For a moment, Tinnie imagined he could still see the outline of his house.

"No. No, I'm not lookin' to sell. Now why would I want to sell? I already got enough of them hot shots in their shiny cars makin' offers."

"Well, I just thought I'd ask. I'm not pushing. You're not looking to rebuild your house, are you?"

"I just might," he imagined aloud. "I just might at that."

"Well, if you decide otherwise I'd appreciate it if you'd call me. Remember, I'm not looking to plant a bunch of houses in your field." The man headed back to his truck. "Next week at noon, right?"

"Yes, that's right," Tinnie responded. "Next week at noon."

"Give my regards to Mrs. Payne for me," he said as he opened the cab door. "How's she doing these days?"

"Nurses almost got her out of bed once this week," Tinnie's voice cracked. "Joints are all crippled up."

"I'm sorry to hear that, Mr. Payne. I really am."

"She'll walk again soon enough. You'll see. They got them some new sort of therapy they's fixin' to do."

"With all that going on I'm surprised you still make it out here every day. You been doing okay yourself now, haven't you?"

"I'm doing just fine, and I don't need no damn nurses. They're there for Millie. They take care of her just fine, and they leave me alone, which is also just fine. They's just a nuisance to me, and I'm no help to them." He stuck a finger in his mouth to rearrange his chew. "Too much for me to do here, anyhow," he added.

"Well, some of us in town worry about you."

"You just mind yourselves. There's already enough worry to go around."

The man climbed into his truck and idled down the hill.

"Don't be late next time," Tinnie called after him. "And you pay care to my driveway."

Tinnie stepped down the familiar trail from the woodpile to the remains of his house and found himself back in his kitchen chair, pondering a new piece of wood he didn't remember picking up.

Could try getting that old International Harvester running, he considered. South field's prime. Damn baler is probably rusted. Never did sell the last bales anyhow. He sliced little ribbons of wood into his hole and eyed the bales of hay, abandoned three years now, half exposed in a warped lean-to shed. Still winded from the walk, he wiped the sweat from his face. Too hot anyhow, he considered. Best do it in the morning, when it's cool.

The shadow of the house cast a darkness over Tinnie. Millie and her pain were fresh on his mind, thanks to the well intentioned man who bought his wood. Well, he thought, I took care of it, that I did. She won't be breaking no more bones on my account. No more creaking floors to worry about.

With tired hands, he folded his knife and admired his stick before tossing it into the cellar. He hobbled to his rust brown '63 Galaxy, rolled it gently down the driveway, and motored a half hour to the assisted living home, which was no more than a brick shoe box with windows. He and Millie and her bad joints lived there with a hundred other variously ailing elderly.

"You get much done today?" Millie slurred, still groggy from her daily pain killers.

"Yes, I did. Sold two cords of wood today," he said, emptying his pockets into a tray on the dresser.

"You swingin' that ax at your age. Lordy me."

Millie's bed was bent into a shallow V, and she asked to be straightened out. She had lost her control.

"I'll get it. I'll get it. Where would you be if I wasn't here to get you out of these fixes? You been folded in half all day?"

"I don't remember. No. Not all day. I don't know."

Tinnie found the control and fumbled with the buttons until the bed hummed itself flat. Millie phased in and out, and often seemed to be in another place.

"You get much done today?" she asked.

"Yes, Millie, I got plenty done today."

After several minutes Millie broke the silence. "You ever get them steps fixed? I won't go back in that house until you get them steps fixed."

"I'm taking care of them. That's not for you to worry about."

"You get them steps fixed, Tinnie, why, we can go on home again. It can be like it was. It's been so long."

Tinnie sat on the edge of his bed, facing away into the antiseptic walls.

"Yes, it has been." His hands, not knowing what to do, rubbed themselves, plowing furrows of loose skin back and forth. "I'll work on them tomorrow."

∞

The next morning was too hot to get the old tractor started. Tinnie planted himself in his chair, pulled out his knife, and began slicing strips of bark off a shaft of dried poplar. He stared into the old foundation as though staring at a ghost. The steps that had needed fixing weighed on his mind.

All her good cooking, he rationalized. She was gaining so much weight back then, that was part of the problem. He had visions of Millie through the years in all her shapes and sizes, but he couldn't be trusted to remember how big she was at the time of her accident. Three years prior she was actually thinning and growing frail, but her plump version best suited Tinnie's reasoning.

Millie's violent fall cast the first shadow over Tinnie. The worst part was that she had warned him. He had felt the spring in the stair himself, but figured if *he* hadn't broken it then it wasn't to be worried about.

And besides, he thought, I had more pressing jobs to get done, and no end to her list of things to do. Her always hounding me, always having to fix this or that. I can only do so much, he would argue. If she'd borne me a child things might have been different. But I'm just one man. Can't very well be at the barn and the house at the same time, now can I?

Tinnie had been on the sunny side of the house, standing on a kitchen chair slopping on a coat of whitewash. Recently split wood was scattered on the hill waiting to be stacked, and the smell of fresh cut hay tickled the air. Then came the entangled crash and scream. The house shuddered under Tinnie's paintbrush. Millie had gone straight through the stairway, a load of laundry in her arms, and landed in a heap in the cellar. With both ankles broken, her right knee cap shattered and hip dislocated, she lay motionless and breathing heavily. Blood flowed from dirty cuts torn by nails and splinters of wood.

The doctors offered little promise. The surgeon who performed the operations explained the extent of the damage and made delicate references to her advanced age. A second doctor told him Millie would probably never walk again. They passed him off to a kindly nurse who gave him shiny pamphlets, referring him to several nursing homes and state support programs.

Tinnie Payne went home that day and stood in front of his worn house, its white washed clapboards peeling away. He'd built it with his own hands over a half century before, anticipating a growing family. It held most of his life and memories, and it was down to its last occupant.

He went to his shed and found the heavy chain he used on uncooperative trees. The old Harvester backfired to a start. He drove to the corner of the house that had already been leaning for a decade and pushed. It went easy, with an impressive crack and several windows shattering. A push from the second corner slid the first floor joists off the foundation, and a portion of the house crashed into the cellar. Tinnie set up his ladder and chained the top of the chimney. On the third pull the stonework smashed through the roof, taking out the ridge and imploding the house. The remaining side walls leaned inward and buckled. The Harvester slid each off the foundation into the enclosing stone walls of the cellar. The little two story farmhouse was reduced to a one story pyre.

Over and over, as he worked, echoing in his mind, "God damn you!"

He marched to his lean-to, grabbed a gas can, tossed the funnel aside, and shook fluid over the fallen walls all the way around the wreckage. It trickled over glass shards and jagged boards, flowing around bits of the past before finally dripping into the cellar. He didn't remember lighting the match.

He found himself kneeling on the cold stone sidewalk, his hat thrown to one side near the overturned kitchen chair. Pamphlets scattered on the ground near his car. Tinnie beat his land with his giant fists as small things fell out of his pockets into the grass.

From the valley floor several new neighbors saw the familiar little white frame house tumble into itself. After several seconds the sound reached them like a prolonged shotgun blast, like a life falling in on itself.

"He must have finally sold out," one woman commented, as flames engulfed the ruin. "Developers don't waste any time, do they?"

∞

FILLING A HOLE

Tinnie whittled his day away, his cane by his side, thinking of all the work that needed to be done. His ancient stone sidewalk needed weeding, and he figured he should do something about getting rid of those old bales of hay, with the south field coming along as it was. But he couldn't bring himself to move from his throne. Little shards of wood went flying free and settled in the ash and weed of the burnt-out cellar. With tight deep eyes no one could see, he kept watch over his vanishing kingdom, ruling by necessity, slowly filling his hole, chip by chip.

The Want of Molly

THE FIRST NIGHT at Aunt Molly's house was not made for sleep. Though the old bungalow creaked and groaned as if it were forever settling, what kept twelve-year-old Aaron awake were his aunt's late night ramblings. Most of what passed through the plaster wall was gibberish, but he could tell by the woman's inflections that she was speaking to some imaginary friend, at times even breaking into spirited debate. On the second night, Aaron stepped into the hall and pressed an ear to her door.

"Men dig," he heard her say. "Always digging. Holes, trenches, ditches. Can't find a man without a shovel in his hand." Aaron waited nervously before knocking, then lurched back as the door swung open. "Whad you want?" his aunt said, her crimped and worried face gaping up at him. Her sleeveless nightgown wasn't much different than the rag-tag line of house dresses she wore every day, and the shallow troughs of skin under her cheeks and upper arms made it look like a great deal of fat had been sucked out of her. Standing there barefoot, toe-to-toe, Aaron noticed for the first time he had grown taller than her.

"I thought I heard you talking to someone," her nephew said, looking past her. The paisley wallpaper made Molly's bedroom vibrate, and the tiny framed pictures of hummingbirds did little to steady the space.

"You see anyone here to be talked to?"

"No ma'am."

"Then I must notta been talking to no one. Now go on. Don't you sleep?"

The boy went back to the guestroom. It would take several more nights of Molly's fidgety tonic of gossip and gab before the house attained a regularity worth sleeping to. The only thing in Molly's room to converse with was a bright-eyed doll peering from a wicker crib, the same crib in which Molly had been laid after her birth forty-seven years ago. Despite a difficult delivery and the uncertain days that followed, she had slept in that same bedroom ever since. It was rumored that Molly was deprived of oxygen for a moment too long. Others figured her problems began at conception.

Aaron's grandfather had bequeathed the old bungalow in town to Molly out of fear of what might become of her. Though Aaron's father was annoyed at the patrimonial slight, his mother didn't seem to mind as she likely feared for her older sister in the same way. She didn't drive, never held a job, and was shaky at best when confronted with multiple choices. The house was within walking distance of the market, the bank, and the post office, which satisfied most of Molly's needs.

Aaron's parents lived three miles out of town on a one acre parcel surrounded by the more weighty farms of the Virginia Piedmont. Demanding both the daily rigor of the urban and the spiritual borderlands of the rural, his father drove forty miles into Washington, D.C. each day to sit behind a government desk and dream of his weekends in the country. The summer Aaron's mother decided to rejoin the workforce, sharing the long commute with her husband to the Patent Office, it was decided that Aaron would be dropped off at his aunt's house each Monday morning to spend the week. The boy fought the idea, claiming he was too old for a baby-sitter. He didn't admit to being slightly afraid of Molly. He wasn't sure what to make of her. Aaron's mother, grasping for justification, claimed that Aunt Molly was the best thing for a boy Aaron's age. Molly could be a second mother to him, she said, though the way she avoided eye contact left her son in doubt.

Aaron assumed Aunt Molly was considered "motherly" because she baked. His own mother had trouble finding the bakery counter in the grocery store, but Molly baked like a woman obsessed. It was her only talent and the one thing she handled with grace. Her house was always filled with the smell of warm bread, cakes, and pastries, most of which were destined for the local market and provided her only trickle of income. A rooster egg timer on the window sill was always diligently set so she wouldn't ruin the sweet-smelling house with the stink of burnt dough and fouled confectionery. Each morning for breakfast she treated Aaron to fresh rye or pumpernickel with elderberry preserves, and throughout the day she fed him treats that his mother would hardly have approved of. In this way, over the first few weeks of summer, Aaron's fear of his aunt waned and morphed into something resembling love.

The house in town was frozen in time from the lean years of their ancestors. Molly was both archivist and housekeeper, a conservator with a dust mop. Though the curtains were threaded from the sun and the ancient lace doilies were dry-rotting on the arms of overstuffed chairs, every flat surface in the house could pass the white-glove test. For Aaron, the house was a history lesson on life in mid-twentieth century America. He listened to dusty 78s of Hank Williams and George Jones on the record phonograph, held his ear to the gothic radio that broadcast only faint winnowy static, and skimmed the library of *Life Magazines* and faceless *National Geographics*.

One day Molly came across Aaron lying on the floor with his nose in an old issue of *Life*, studying the Zapruder series of the Kennedy assassination with a magnifying glass. Molly stood over him as he examined each frame with eager eyes, searching for pieces of the president's brain exploding across the image. There was no way to sanitize something so public and violent from the innocent eyes of a twelve-year-old boy. Aaron wondered of the president's last thought as the bullet passed through his head, and what sensation, if any, he might have felt. He wondered the same of the president's wife as she climbed frantically over the trunk of the limo. The killing was all at once very real to Aaron and provided an excitement he hadn't known before.

Molly said, "They done got him good, didn't they." The boy looked over his shoulder and saw her there in the same kind of lazy house dress she wore every day.

"Do you remember it?" Aaron asked.

"Wasn't but a dozen years ago. Lost his head the same month your momma birthed you." She started back to the kitchen to inspect an oven full of rising banana bread. "Guess it all evened out," she added, trailing off.

She had a closet full of those smock-like dresses, and Aaron wondered if it wasn't by design they resembled nightgowns. Several times each day he would find her dozing, sitting upright on either the sofa or the splintery porch swing where she waited for the rooster egg-timer to wake her. The way her shoulders dipped and mouth hung open made her look like she'd given up on a part of her life. But what made her naps unsettling was that she slept with her eyes open, always a spooked gaze as if she were trying to penetrate some other dimension.

Aaron spent most afternoons that summer with his friend Mitch Harris, either tooling around the back alleys of town or trespassing up and down the Cole Creek Valley. They spent the long summer days hardening their lungs with stolen cigarettes, lighting things on fire to see how they burned, and inventing games of questionable legality. Mitch's father owned a used car dealership in the county seat, and was as known for making deals as for sleeping with the long line of secretaries that had worked under his predatory gaze. Aaron knew Mitch was afraid of him. He had witnessed the man's two personas and it was impossible to predict which one would show up – the one who tried to ingratiate himself with the local boys by telling foul-mouth jokes, some of which the youngsters didn't fully understand, or the one who would greet Mitch with a violent back-hand across the face. Mitch's mother, a waifish soul possessing no more kindness than meanness, busied herself corralling Mitch's three younger siblings and cashing her husband's checks. She was partial to the ease of low expectations, and her eldest son was happy to accommodate her.

Aaron and Mitch's favorite pastime was tormenting the town bum. They found him one day loitering on the corner of Westbury and Chapel, wearing a nylon ski cap turned up over the brow and a surplus camouflage overcoat that was several sizes too large. Mitch had brought a pocket full of dried up horse turds from a farmer's field (he was handy that way), and chucked one at the bum, thumping him upside the head. The man's reaction was subdued, his speech mottled as if he had no tongue, though it was there in plain sight, resting on his lower lip like a raw hamburger patty. He came at them slow and clumsy, his face down as if forced to plan each step. His stride was like that of a naked man running over sharp rocks.

Mitch yelled, "Incoming!" and released a barrage of turds into the air. The boys peed their pants as they ran away.

The bum's proper name was Aubrey, but anyone who called him anything called him Mumbles. The town's inhabitants referred to him as "our bum," not out of any sense of indentured servitude or that he somehow belonged to them, but that he had earned a place in the community, a tolerated place where he wasn't perceived as a threat. Or perhaps it was just a way to say that the position of town bum was occupied and there was no room for another. So long as he was *their* bum, their *only* bum, Mumble's position was secure and the town accepted him with a steady endurance, like it would a leaning lamp post or a root-cracked sidewalk. No one seemed to know where Aubrey came from, and it was doubtful anyone could have understood him had he offered up the information. One could only guess his age. Some said he was about fifty, but this number didn't fit with the older folks in town who said he had always been there, like the grain elevator or the railroad. Whatever the number, the years did not play well on him.

Aubrey fished Cole Creek every day for anything that was biting, usually catfish or small-mouth bass, but in the lengthening drought that summer his prey settled downstream in the warm brown backwater of the Cawhauler dam. It was too far to walk, especially through the dense brush and thickets on the creek's muddy banks, so Aubrey was more dependent than usual on the generosity of the townsfolk. The local grocer, to whom Molly sold her baked goods, always left a handful of slightly expired fruit or vegetables in the alley next to the dumpster, and those in town who occasionally hired Aubrey for odd jobs around their yards (never inside) were inclined to prepare him a bag lunch.

When Aunt Molly informed Aaron she'd hired Mumbles to paint her house and that he was expected to help, Aaron was suffused in a preteen windstorm of dread and embarrassment. Like all young boys at one time or another, he wanted to flee, to break from the threat of shame and responsibility, and leave town with all his belongings tied to the end of a stick. Then he whiplashed to the other extreme and promised to paint the whole house by himself.

Molly shoveled off a dozen oatmeal-raisin cookies from her baking sheet, shaking her head. "You can't paint the whole house. You're too small."

"I am not. I promise I'll do it."

"I'm gonna buy two of everything. Two scrapers, two brushes, and two'a dem funny painter hats."

"Then I got stuff I gotta do," Aaron pleaded, almost in tears.

She waved her spatula at him.

"You ain't got no stuff that I can see."

The torments of Mumbles were a constant that summer, and Aaron began assembling a time-line of the minor atrocities he and Mitch had inflicted on him. Only the day before, Mitch had hit the poor bum square in the back with a water balloon, and by the time Mumbles turned around, Mitch was long gone, leaving Aaron doubled over and giggling in his wake. Mitch never said what he was going to do next, or when, and now Aaron, who was usually little more than an accomplice, was growing wary of his friend's casual cruelty.

The next day Aaron escorted his aunt arm-in-arm to the paint store where she pestered the manager for an hour over brush types, rollers, cleaning agents, and an infinite array of color samples. Molly was not good with choices. The next afternoon a delivery truck pulled up to her house and a man unloaded a canvas drop-cloth, two scrapers, two wide synthetic brushes, two cans of turpentine, ten gallons of primer, and another ten gallons of flat white paint onto her porch. Molly signed the receipt by making her mark, a scribbly "M" that could have been read as a "W." The delivery man carried his clipboard back to the truck, shaking his head.

When Aubrey came to Molly's house that first morning in mid-July, he lingered on the back porch for an hour without knocking. Aaron, still in his pajamas, peeked from the upstairs bedroom and saw him coming up the lawn, then burrowed back under the covers and played dead, dreading the first awkward encounter and fearing the bum might smack him at first sight.

After a while the boy thought Aubrey might have left, perhaps after seeing all the work that was going to be required. The house was peeling badly, right to the bare wood, but it was not likely Mumbles was intimidated as he was sometimes hired by the local farmers to do some of the foulest jobs in the valley. No one in the county shoveled shit so well and without protest, and had anyone else crawled under a sty with the droppings and doodies of five thousand chickens, they might have eagerly shot themselves in the head the same evening. But Mumbles always worked dutifully and without complaint. It's doubtful a little peeling paint even fazed him. The more likely reason he loitered on Molly's porch that morning was the smell of her early batch of bread still raising its tender crown, seeping through the windows and circling the house like a warm embrace. It was doubtful Aubrey was used to such things, though it might have reminded him of an earlier time.

Molly eventually found Aubrey when she went out to hang laundry. She hollered for Aaron, who lumbered out in his pajama bottoms, thinking he might be less likely to be struck if only half clothed. To his surprise, Mumbles regarded him as he would a pumpkin or a bush. At first the boy thought he was being shunned, but then noticed the dirty man was staring at his aunt in a kind of befuddled longing. The only hint of emotion was in his eyes as he took in the chattering woman and the smell from her oven. Aunt Molly seemed oblivious to his gaze and went about giving painfully long and incoherent instructions of how she wanted the house painted. Then without warning, Aubrey broke from his trance, picked up a shiny new scraper, and went to work on a short section of wall by the chimney. Molly rambled on for another minute before shooing Aaron off to get dressed and fed. Before going inside, she pondered her help for a moment, watching him scrape hard on the first board. "I'm going to bake you a cake," she exclaimed, before tromping off to the kitchen.

Aaron stalled as long as he could before taking his place on the other side of the chimney. Together he and Aubrey worked the short end of the house, shearing the dry chips of paint off the clapboard in white explosions under the ring of the metallic scrapers. The boy neglected the areas of paint that clung stubbornly to the siding, but Aubrey had a different approach, working methodically, scraping only one board at a time and refusing to move on until there was nothing left but the chalky wood grain. He was slow but thorough. They worked together those first few weeks with the chimney separating them, giving Aaron time and space to acclimate to his strange new workmate. Once they turned the corner, they worked side-by-side over the hatch to the cellar as Aaron watched Aubrey's puffy hands scrape away the generations. Not once did they speak, though in time they worked together like old friends who were no longer embarrassed by silence. Aubrey came and went on his own schedule, usually working for several hours each morning and leaving only after Molly had set him up with a bag of sandwiches and cookies. Then he would take his lunch and disappear into the valley to fish and sleep under the sycamores, dreaming his unimaginable dreams.

∞

The land was owned by the railroad and the barn was surplus property long forgotten by the Norfolk Southern. Railroad ties smelling thick of creosote were stacked unevenly against the barn and scattered around the yard among pieces of rusty equipment that were past their useful lives. Mitch rattled the pad lock on the first door of the barn, but the metal had long since fused together. On the back side, away from the rails and behind a thicket of briars, he spotted the top half of a Dutch door, and it didn't take him long to find the trampled path burrowing under the bramble to the door's base. The two friends crawled on their hands and knees, and when they got to the bottom half of the door, they pulled it open and felt the cool mildewy air touch their faces.

Once inside, Mitch kicked along like he had been there many times before, but to Aaron this felt like a home invasion, no different from prowling inside a neighbor's house. He took silent steps as he acclimated to the light, feeling his way along the hay dust and compacted earth. He was afraid to move anything or to leave a trace that he had been there. Mitch swaggered ahead, inspecting the line of abandoned stalls until he came to one where the straw had been brushed aside and the dirt floor swept clear. On one side, organized neatly on a wooden crate, was a bum's kitchen: stacked cans of Sterno, matches, a crusted frying pan and boiling pot, plastic bags of half-eaten baked goods, and a plastic tray containing a bent fork, a spoon, and a variety of dull knives. In the crate were expired cans of cream corn, string beans, and a near empty bottle of Mad Dog 20-20. Mitch hopped over the gate. Aaron was taken by his profile. There was some new twist to his face, something resembling hate.

Mitch stared at the little pantry. "This is pathetic," he said. Before Aaron could see what he had found, Mitch kicked the crate and sent the cans, pots, and utensils strewing across the stall. He stomped on a can of cream corn as Aaron climbed onto the gate.

"Stop it," Aaron said, jumping down to the hard-pack. He recognized the bread bags as the ones his aunt used.

Mitch stalked across the stall, picked up a dented can of Sterno, and put it in his pocket. "What a loser," he said. In the next stall he found a woolen nest of blankets over a thick bed of straw. Above were several more threaded covers folded neatly in the hay loft. Somewhere between rage and glee, Mitch jumped the fence and went about wrecking Aubrey's bed. He stomped and twisted in a kind of epileptic dance before kicking the crap out of the bedding, sending wads of moldy blanket and straw in all directions. He didn't stop until Aaron caught him off balance and shoved him to the ground.

"Knock it off," Aaron cried.

Mitch fell against the feed stall where his hand went through the collar and came down on something tin and hollow. Instead of taking a swing at Aaron, he rolled onto his knees and reached into the trough where he retrieved a metal tin with a marlin on the cover. His face turned greedy as he placed it in the middle of Aubrey's wrecked bed and flipped off the top.

"Put it back," Aaron told him. "It's his stuff."

Like a conquistador searching for gold with the tip of his sword, Mitch started tossing things out of the box with no more than a cursory inspection, passing on the few things in the poor man's life that might have value to him: a deck of cards, a metal button, rusty fishing hooks, seashell fossils, a dozen foil gum wrappers, a perfectly shaped acorn, a mercury dime. At the bottom were two pages torn from an early Playboy Magazine, and Mitch quickly stuffed them in his pocket. Then they saw the photograph. Lying in the bottom of the desecrated tin was a small black and white of a young woman, and it took them a few seconds to recognize who it was.

"That's your aunt." Mitch said.

"It is not," Aaron countered, not quite believing himself.

"Mumbles is laying your Aunt!"

Aaron wanted to punch the bastard. "She is not!" he yelled back. "She just feeds him."

"Uncle Mumbles."

"Screw you."

Aaron took a swing, but Mitch had been so toughened by his father's backhands that Aaron's unimpressive fist made little impression. That wasn't their first fight that summer, as they were in that childish he-man mode of fighting over just about anything, but this one struck Aaron as worth fighting for. The presence of Molly's photo among the bum's trinkets stunned his feeble preteen reasoning. Though Mitch had proven nothing, his accusation had a ring of truth to it. As Aaron lie on his back shielding Mitch's overhand blows, his mind focused on the image of his aunt. The photo had a serrated edge that was popular in the fifties and was of Molly in the spring of her adult years. She had the same bewildered face, but looked vaguely pretty in a way her nephew had never imagined. Her eyes still had that restless quality, but her gaze showed greater interest in life and whatever was in front of her, a kind of interest Aaron had never before seen in her. If Molly had ever loved, this photo might have captured that brief magical time.

His first theory was that Aubrey had snuck into his aunt's house and stolen the photo, but he quickly dismissed the idea as he couldn't see the man doing anything subversive. He also knew that his aunt, ever concerned for her privacy, would never let a man into her house, especially a man like Aubrey. People would talk. It wouldn't be proper. Though there was never a hint that Molly and Aubrey had known each other in their youth, there was no evidence to show they hadn't. The only other theory was that Molly had given Aubrey the photo.

∞

Aaron slept on a sofa-bed in the upstairs sitting room next to a bookcase lined with the brittle spines of old hardbacks: *A Tree Grows in Brooklyn*, *Migratory Birds of the East Coast*, and *The First Thanksgiving*. The only interesting part of the room was what came through the walls on a nightly basis, and now his aunt's jabbering was coming later each evening in ever-rising distress. She had changed the delivery schedule of her baked goods from morning to evening, wheeling her cart the three blocks to the back of Caldwell's grocery near closing time, and each evening she came home a little later. She claimed it was the only cool part of the day for her to walk and get her exercise. The night Aaron heard her flat-footed steps come through the back door at eleven-thirty, he placed a milk glass against the wall and waited for Molly to close her bedroom door.

"Men beg," her muffled voice carried. "Always beggin'. Beggin' them things ain't proper." She paused, and this time Aaron could hear her labored breathing. "One track mind, I tell you." The floor creaked under her nervous pacing. "Can't be doing that. No, sir. Not proper." Her voice was shrill, and caused in Aaron a rising anxiety as he pressed his ear into the glass.

∞

Three square windows were lined up across the long side of the barn, and the lamplight from inside glowed brightest from the center. The night was black, but for the red and green lights on the nearby switching tower. The air was so thick with humidity it choked out all but the brightest stars. The boys stood tiptoe on the poorly stacked railroad ties that wobbled beneath their feet, and they gripped the window trim with their fingertips. Inside, the light from a kerosene lamp made the horizontal boards of the stall glow yellow, while the rest of the space receded in varying shades of darkness, like a chapel lit in solemn Mass. The two boys looked down and saw them there on the rebuilt bedding. She was spread out on her back like she'd fallen from a great height. The loose jiggling flesh of her arms and legs were all of her they could see as he was on top, his hunched and hairy back pushing between her legs in a kind of hemorrhage and making a sound like Aaron had once heard from the walrus tank at the zoo. Their bodies were all tensed up and flabby at the same time. Like some instinctive animal, Aubrey never stopped his manic attack, pounding ever harder into the flabby frame of Molly. Aaron was afraid he might break her, and was absorbed in shame and confusion as the sound of the katydids merged with the thrusting of Mumbles. His grip on the window sill loosened from the shock of what he was seeing.

"Holy crap," Mitch said. As he pressed his nose on the glass, the stack of ties shifted and sent the boys tumbling to the ground. They scraped and bloodied their shins and forearms, but felt little as they jumped up and ran along the tracks toward town. Mitch followed him up the street laughing hysterically. Aaron was near tears.

"Go home," Aaron said. "Stop following me."

"I want something to eat."

"Beat it!"

Mitch kept after him, perhaps knowing he would get his way. They ended up on Molly's back porch munching from a tin of molasses cookies. Mitch examined his wounds as Aaron stared quietly across the yard.

"So has he been here?" Mitch asked. "In her bedroom?"

"No. I'da heard them."

"She must want it bad to do it with Mumbles."

"What do you know about girls?"

"As much as you, shit-for-brains." Mitch noticed the paint cans, then motioned toward the brushes soaking in a mason jar filled with spirits.

"What's that stuff?" he asked.

∞

The usual August drought settled on the Piedmont, counting thirty days since the last rain. Yards were chapped and brown with only weeds seeming to thrive, and the ground had shrunken back from the sidewalks leaving gaps wide enough mice to crawl. The whole state was a tinderbox, so it was no surprise when one Saturday morning the valley caught fire.

It started near town on the shallow side of the tracks where the tall brush lay on its side. The flames spread up the valley to the northeast where they devoured fifty acres of pasture, four barns, two resident thoroughbreds, and the house of Bill and Mandy Picket. The fire chief was the first to find the charred remains of Mandy and her infant daughter in the room where they had been napping.

The first thing that had burned was the abandoned barn near the tracks where piles of creosote soaked railroad ties smoldered for two days. All that was left of the barn was the cinder block foundation. Nearby lay an empty gallon tin of turpentine and a can of Sterno.

∞

Molly was asleep on the sofa when the sheriff knocked on her back door. She dawdled to the door where she found the uniformed man looking over her paint supplies. The air was tinted with a residue of smoke and stink that made Molly raise her nose and grimace. She stood there wringing her hands in her apron, blinking those eyes that never rested, while the sheriff studied the label and batch number of the can of turpentine.

"Miss. Blount," he said, still squinting at the can, "I'm Sheriff Clayton."

"I see who you are. You think I'm blind?"

"No ma'am, I'm sure you can see just fine." He looked up and regarded her like he would a child. "I understand you hired Aubrey Koop to paint your house."

"He does. He paints my house." She crimped her nose. "What's that stink?"

"Has he been by today?"

"He ain't got no schedule. He comes when he wants."

"Then you haven't seen him today?"

"I ain't seen no one but you snooping round my porch."

The sheriff touched the brim of his hat and stepped into the grass before turning back. "I hope you don't mind, but I'll need to borrow this." He held up the can of solvent.

"I paid good money for that."

"I understand. I'll reimburse you myself if I have to. Now you'll call me if Aubrey shows up, won't you?"

"I might."

"Miss. Blount, it's important I talk to him. I need to find him before someone else does."

The sheriff walked back to his car, leaving Molly tasting the acrid air and muttering to herself. "Men take," she said, wriggling her nose. "Always taking."

∞

Aaron was home with his parents the weekend of the fire and overheard his father on the phone. When told about the Picket family, his father let out a groan and shook his head. Then he spoke Aubrey's name and shook his head again. After hanging up, Aaron asked him what happened.

"There was a terrible fire near town," his father said, and then explained about the Pickets. "That's all we know."

"Was Aubrey hurt?"

His father paused and stared into his mother's stricken face.

"He doesn't seem to be around to ask."

Aaron telephoned Mitch, but his family was busy packing the car for a two-week vacation to Virginia Beach. Mitch said he'd seen the fire up close, but was hesitant to give much detail. It was old news to him now, and he didn't want to talk about it. But there was something more in his voice, a kind of nervous urgency to get off the phone and get out of town. His father was yelling in the background, hurling beach chairs and insults. Aaron was soon left with a dial-tone.

The boy was anxious to be dropped off at his aunt's house Monday morning so he could walk the valley, see the destruction, and feel the place where people had died. He dropped his things at Molly's house and ran back out with such excitement that he didn't notice his aunt sitting at the dining room table, a place where she never sat. She didn't say hello or goodbye, and never even offered him breakfast. Aaron ran out the door without noticing her idle kitchen.

The boy crossed the tracks and stopped on the rise where he surveyed the charred corner of the valley. The pungent air infected his nostrils as he stepped into the burnt grasses. Through the blackened sticks of the cedars, he spotted the foundation of the barn, its cinder block imprint cordoned off with yellow police tape. The piles of ties were still giving off a whither of smoke. Any evidence of the origin of the blaze had been removed to the sheriff's office. He wandered a few hundred yards across the ashen landscape and came to the skeletal remains of the Picket's house. He tried to imagine these two people he did not know burning like sacrifices by the marauding flames, the warmth of their home turning into some fantastic funeral pyre. He wondered if either Mandy or her daughter had woken, and he wondered of their last thoughts, or if they had had any thoughts at all. For Aaron there was an odd thrill of being there, the thrill of seeing tragedy and trying to understand without actually having to suffer for it.

When he got back to his aunt's house the door was locked, and for the first time he had to use his key to get inside. Molly was back on the couch in her usual wide-eyed sleeping pose, but he could tell she was not asleep. Her eyes showed great concentration, as if she were trying to levitate something before her. Then he noticed the house's lack of bakery appeal, and he knew something was wrong.

"Aunt Molly," he said, approaching cautiously from one side. "Are you okay?"

"Whad you want?" she answered, still staring ahead.

"Has Aubrey been by?"

"Hush yourself. Can't you be quiet?" She turned her hands over and back again. "Boy's always asking questions."

Aaron backed away. "I'm gonna get some breakfast."

Some alarm seemed to go off in Molly's head, and she rushed to the kitchen, giving him a chill as she brushed past.

"Get yourself outta my kitchen. I'm feeding you. You just wait. Can't you wait?" She scrambled around the counters in a desperate huff, dropping an odd mix of things from the cabinets that satisfied no single recipe. Aaron went to the next room to watch the black and white tv and tried to block out his aunt's manic and pointless racket. An hour later he found her back on the porch swing, though she was not swinging. She seemed afraid to move, as if any motion might attract unwanted attention. Her usually orderly kitchen was now a flower dusted confusion of mixing bowls, pans, and spilled cooking oils. Aaron made himself a bowl of cereal and snatched a handful of cookies, and did the same for dinner as he left his aunt to her thoughts. He was scared for her and considered calling his mother for help, but decided instead to respect his aunt's privacy.

He waited that evening for her mottled speech through the wall, hoping to learn what was wrong, but she never came to bed. All he heard was her pacing the floor below. When the back door slammed shut, he went to the window and lifted the screen. Directly below he could see her in the shadows coming around the side of the house. She worked the pad lock on the hatch to the cellar, heaved open the door, and began speaking into the hole as if having one of her bedroom conversations. But this time a voice spoke back – a series of grunts waxing from the blackness.

Aaron rushed downstairs, slid out the back door, and tiptoed across the porch. He didn't know what he was going to do. He just felt like he should be there for them. As he came to the overgrown boxwoods at the corner of the house, three beams of light flashed across the lawn from different directions and heavy footsteps tromped up the driveway and rustled through the hedgerow of the neighbor's lot. Aaron dropped to his knees and pressed into the bushes as Molly spun around and let out a shriek. A hand clasped over her mouth as two other men lit the cellar and found their prey. They pulled Aubrey from the abyss by his arms and hair, and he cowered under their blows like he'd been beaten many times in his life. Molly kicked hard to break away, but the man held her steady. His large hand covered most of her face, and fallen threads of hair obscured her eyes. He told the others to stop beating Aubrey, that there was no time for that now, as he led Molly past the boxwoods to the back door and forced her inside. Aaron's body was all seized up as he listened to the men talking.

"We shoulda waited 'til that crazy woman went to bed," one man said.

"I told you she had the key. Now keep him quiet."

One of the men wrapped a piece of clothes line around Aubrey's face, cinching it through his mouth. The bum huddled on his knees with a wet stain on his crotch and drool running down his chin, bracing for the next blow. The door to the house closed, and the man who had escorted Molly inside flashed a beam of light once over Aaron's head. A car came up the street with its headlights off, and as it pulled into the driveway all three men dragged Aubrey over and heaved him into the back seat. Aaron recognized the driver's face under the burning dome light as a schoolmate's father whose surname was Picket. The car and its band of men quietly rolled away.

Aaron stayed on his hands and knees under the boxwood trembling uncontrollably, trying to squeeze down the fear, but he kept replaying the scene over and over, frame-by-frame. It was not a thrill, but a quiet terror. Afraid to leave the safety of his burrow, afraid more men might be watching and waiting, he considered staying there all night. He even considered walking the three miles of dark highway to his parent's house. He finally crawled out from the brush and crept onto the back porch where he peeked through the window. Molly was sitting on the kitchen floor with her back to the cabinets, her cheek pressed awkwardly against one shoulder. Her eyes were barely open, and the erratic spirit that once shone from them had dimmed. Aaron tried the door, but it was locked. He swallowed hard and tapped on the window.

"Aunt Molly." His breath fogged a little patch on the glass. "It's me. Can you open the door?" He rapped a little harder. "Can you please open the door?"

∞

The newspaper said Aubrey drowned in six inches of water. That was all the drought had left in Cole Creek that August, the rest having drained off toward the Chesapeake or evaporated into the very air the townsfolk breathed. He had apparently slipped on a rock and taken a blow to the head. There was no mention of a funeral. It was as if he'd just moved on to another town and became someone else's bum. Only years later did Aaron wonder where people like Aubrey were laid to rest.

The night of Aubrey's death was the last Aaron spent at his aunt's house. Aunt Molly, he was told, was suddenly too busy to handle him. Her needs had changed, though he knew she had lost her head.

Molly spent two months in a state mental hospital and suffered a series of "treatments" that were never fully revealed to Aaron. When she was allowed to go home, she was incapable of speech and was prone to bouts of violent shaking and paranoia. From then on Molly would see only Aaron's mother. She filed Molly's disability papers, brought her groceries, filled her many prescriptions, hired a lawn service, and convinced the Post Master to hand-deliver the mail to her door. She made sure all of Molly's needs were cared for, though her wants were not apparent. Molly no longer had the drive to spend her days baking. Her dutiful sister, likely exhausted by her new responsibilities, simply blamed it on the new medications.

Aaron kept his promise to his aunt to paint her house, though he did so slowly, coming the next four summers by bike and eventually by car to do small sections at a time, each in the thorough and tedious way he had learned from watching Aubrey's swollen hands do their work. Not once did Molly greet him. But though the blinds were always drawn, he frequently felt watched, and a few times he caught Molly's wide eye peering from behind a pinch of drapery. That was as close to her as he could get.

When he finally finished painting the house, Aaron felt pride in what he had done – caring for his ailing aunt, paying homage to a homeless man, and adding his own generational layer to the old bungalow. But his pride was suffused with the guilt of having done nothing to help Molly and her late beau on the night of the kidnaping. And now that guilt was all the more bitter as he looked closely at the wall by the chimney where he and Aubrey had first worked side-by-side. The paint was beginning to peel.

Against his mother's wishes, Aaron decided to see his Aunt again face-to-face, to get her attention and tell her how sorry he was for what had happened and how he missed her strange ways. He went to her house at an odd hour and caught her outside, though still out of sight of the townsfolk, sitting on the back porch staring blankly at pictures in an old magazine. When she saw the front end of Aaron's car nose into the backyard, she jumped up and scurried into the house with her smock trailing behind her. The floor boards of the old porch creaked under Aaron's feet as he came to the door. He knocked and called her name, but heard only her footsteps trailing off somewhere deep inside, somewhere to rest, perhaps, and close her eyes.

Reappraising Jason

JASON STOPPED HIS BMW dead on the road in front of his appointment and balanced his steaming coffee on the wheel. Christ, this has to be a foreclosure, he thought. It's bad enough I'm drawing all the crap assignments this week, but now they've got me back in this rural ghetto again. They didn't even give me a heads-up.

He sat his coffee on the dash and picked up his clipboard to begin taking notes, but he wasn't sure where to begin. His first impression was of the multiple colors of shingles in abstract patterns; the original layer was indiscernible. The left side of the roof was concave and the ridge seemed only to hang on the smoking brick chimney, without which the structure would implode. The house didn't stand proudly, but lay on the ground like an old sleeping dog.

He looked over the bank's appraisal order. It gave no clue of the purpose of the report, but he knew bankrupt farmers were scattered about and not so amiable to men in suits who drive fast cars. He had once been escorted off another property by an impoverished and well-armed landowner.

Jason had spent his youth in this corner of the county, a good portion of it trying to get out. His family estate, a dirt farm with no end of labor, was more burden than legacy. He considered the day his brother bought him out as the day he could start to make something of himself.

Okay, it's simple, he thought. I've dealt with these before. The plan is to get in and out as fast as possible; to step on no toes.

Since the driveway resembled the roof, with at least three types of paving in a mosaic of ice-glazed craters, he parked on a strip of firm ground adjacent to the mailbox. The engine died to the barking of two mixed breeds as they splashed through half frozen puddles down the driveway. Jason threw open the door and lowered his voice, "get back, go on now . . . get back." The dogs held their ground as Jason stiff-armed them with his clipboard. Then a crusty voice called down the driveway.

"Hey now Murray! Rummy! C'mon, get on back here! Get on back here now. C'mon. Get on back." The dogs yielded with suspicion and circled behind their master. "Hey there now. It's okay. They don't bite none. They's just loud, that's all. You Mr. Durham? You the appraiser?"

A tall black man of sixty-odd years loomed large in front of Jason's car. His face of deep-carved lines mirrored years of hard work, but the creases bent around his mouth in a wry smile that gave him the gentle air of a preacher. His green work pants and mustard coat reminded Jason again of his roof, with multiple patches and fissures.

"Yes sir. I'm Jason Durham. I see you have a good security system here."

"Yes suh, yes suh. They is that and more trouble."

Jason feared he was being studied the same way he had scrutinized the old man's house. He wore the hot-shot banker style with a cashmere coat exposing only a silk knot. For his own protection he had learned not to overdress for, what he called, "special deals." Low key was usually best when it came to foreclosures, but it was too late for that. He thought a little dirt on his sleeve or leather shoes might make them both feel more at ease. He straightened his coat and extended his hand. Calloused but soft, the old man's palm swallowed his, leaving only the pink tip of Jason's thumb exposed.

"I'm Ray Trammel. I'm pleased to meet yuh." He guided their hands up and down before giving Jason a serious eye. "Now what all is it the bank needs you to do here today?"

"I just need to see the house, walk the land, and take a couple of pictures. It shouldn't take more than a few minutes of your time."

The air was full of frozen breath and burning firewood, and the ashen sky had grown heavy, waiting to drop the first snow. Jason felt the chill in his lungs and slicked back hair as his senses sharpened. He snapped a photograph of the house and walked along the edge of the driveway with Mr. Trammel a long stride behind. He instinctively began with his usual questions. "So, have you made any recent improvements to your property?" After the words left his lips, his mouth lingered open in regret.

"Yes suh. I done all sorts of stuff here," Ray said, waving his hand high in blessing. "Yuh see, I patched all the roof . . . n'up there too, yuh see, by the chimney? Had some leakin' up there last summer n'I took care of that." He gestured to the crinkled aluminum flashing and dripping caulk against the cracked masonry. "You wanna see inside too?" Ray led the way to the stoop and pulled open the screen door with no screen. The front door settled as it cleared the jamb. "Now what is it all you wanna see? This here's the living room."

Upon crossing the threshold, Jason was thawed by what felt like a blast furnace in a steel mill. The chimney, which was the last linchpin that kept the house above the horizon, also anchored a large and effective wood burning stove. The surrounding walls had no more than a few square feet of smooth plaster under peeling paint and wallpaper, and the ceiling reflected the repairs to the roof, with numerous intersecting brown circles.

Ray lifted and slammed the door behind them as the dogs raced across the threaded remnants and curled up on an overstuffed chair in the farthest corner from the fireplace.

"Nellie, this here's Mr. Durham. He's sent by the bank to see the house."

Nellie peered through an opening in the nearest wall and stared at Jason, who was now scribbling furiously on his clipboard. She nodded and returned to her cooking. Nellie hunched over an iron stove in a shapeless garment, half dress, half smock, with the hem and several threads dangling to the floor. She rocked from side-to-side in rhythm with the stir of her stew.

The smell from her cooker woke Jason from his scribbling and began flooding him with boyhood memories of his mother's kitchen. Always a commotion, with stifling heat and perspiring walls, every inch of counter space busy. His mother would often sing quietly to herself, which had a calming effect on all the activity, and at the same time made the kitchen the soul of the house. Her own stews were the culmination of months of the family's sweat. At the dinner table Jason would plod and play, using his spoon to segregate each vegetable he had helped plant, pick, shuck, peel and snap. But somewhere between his hours of labor and the culinary reward, he not only lost interest, but he became resentful. He couldn't remember why. The last time he had returned to the remains of his family's farm, it certainly wasn't for the food. Somewhere along his path the flavor changed; the appreciation faded. The smell of Nellie's stew made him crave a taste of it again, as though he knew some forgotten thing would rush back to him. To restore in him something he had lost or long ago fled.

"Nice to meet you," Jason said, craning his neck to follow the scent.

"Is'e gonna stay for suppa?" Nellie asked.

"Well now, he can stay if he wants," Ray hollered back. "You got plenty back there don'tcha?"

"Oh, no thank you, Mr. Trammel. It sure smells good, but I just need to inspect the house and I'll be on my way."

"We got more'n we can eat," Nellie added.

"Uh, no, really, I'll just be a few minutes," Jason said, wavering between the allure of the stew and the repulsion of the house. Ray walked his long stride across the living room. Jason put the stew out of his mind and followed with the clipboard shielding his right side from the blast furnace. They stopped in the tiny hallway.

"We got two bedrooms back here. And we got a bathroom too," Ray said, pushing open the first door.

Relieved at the indoor plumbing, Jason stepped under Ray's extended arm into the dampness. He flipped the light switch and the bulb over the sink surged and dimmed. Rusty Venetian blinds tangled with curtain and towel to choke out any light from the window. As he turned to leave, his coat snagged the half-open medicine cabinet door, pulling it wide to reveal a flower of razor blades blooming from the rear disposal slot.

He sidestepped into the hall as Ray pushed open the two bedroom doors. Jason glanced into the first bedroom, then followed a commotion from the second where there was nowhere to stand except the two-foot arc of the door swing. Dressers and piles of clothes lined the walls, and a bed sagged in the middle of the room. A boy in a Bulls jersey was wedged between a dresser and the bed, inches from a TV, wrestling with a joystick in a game of *Mortal Kombat*. He turned toward Jason, revealing nothing in his eyes.

"Hi," Jason offered.

The boy turned back to his game and said "hi" to the monitor. Jason felt a touch of familiarity with the boy, but he couldn't place it. He knew he had never seen him before. He stepped back into the hall as the door drifted shut, pinching off the game's artificial cries.

"And this down here is the kitchen."

"Mr. Trammel, I'll need to see your furnace."

"You didn't feel it when you came in?" he said, showing a silvery grin. He led Jason to a closet next to the stove and unstuck the door. "I got this here one a few years back from a house they tore down to build the new bypass. Ain't hooked up. Ain't got no use for it yet. Maybe if I run outta wood some day, I'll use it."

Jason guessed it was a twenty-year-old gas furnace. He knew there were no gas lines available in these parts, and his mind started reeling with federal minimum property standards, and the health and building code violations. Then he figured the bank will get stuck with the house and probably level it anyway.

Ray shut the closet door revealing Nellie still stirring her bubbling cooker. The wallpaper over her stove resembled flypaper and Jason had an image that the grease, in agreement with the chimney, might have a role in buttressing the house.

"Well, that should take care of the inside," said Jason.

"That's it? Can't I at least get you something to drink?" Ray asked. He had a proud eye on his new refrigerator, the crown jewel of the estate.

"No thanks. You want to show me around the lot?" Jason had seen more than he wanted and motioned to the back door.

"Hold on. That door don't work so well. Let me show you the way." Ray guided Jason to the front door as he said goodbye and thank you again to Mrs. Trammel, all the while sensing memories from her cooker. Nellie still swayed from side to side in time as her stew stirred and bubbled. As he passed, Jason heard an almost inaudible sound, like a quiet hymn, coming from this small woman.

Ray pulled the door open with a thud as it bounced off the floor and dragged over the carpet. The screen door was open and the dogs bounced back to life, happy to cool off again.

"Did yuh see the new ice box?"

"Oh yes, I took note of it," Jason replied, feigning interest. "So, you have five acres here?" When they circled the house he noticed that the entire rear wall was re-covered with aluminum siding. The back door and bathroom window weren't even there, apparently covered and sealed by Ray's handiwork.

"Yuh see that tree, the big one with the black bark? Then the little one to the left of it? Right there's one corner. N'back yonder past my pile is a stake. You can't see it from here, but that's the other corner."

The pines creaked overhead as Jason stood among months of dead weeds and years of debris. Between Ray and his pile was some standing water of greenish pulp and more scant trees, some leaning and tired; some already retired to the ground. This was Ray's central heating system. Jason wondered if the trees would last until the gas company laid their lines. Around them several ancient vehicles in colors of primer were scattered and abandoned; their potential lay rusting and storing an abundance of things of no value. Jason locked his eyes on a frozen tractor and plow engulfed in honeysuckle vine, causing his mind to wander again. He looked away from Ray.

This was the way it always was, he thought, recalling his old family farm. Something was always broken, breaking down, or falling apart. You work your ass off and you get the same dead tractor. The same curling shingles. Things to do piling up all around and never enough time. All we ever did was fight over what needed to get done first. So what's the old man going to do with all this crap? Just him and that kid and everything falling apart. What value could he possibly place on these things?

"Well, Mr. Trammel, that's all I need to see." Jason started back to his car, still avoiding eye contact. Nellie's stew had been forgotten and he was glad to be moving on.

"That's it, uh? Well, that wasn't so bad. So what you figure it's worth? Am I gonna be a millionaire?" Ray showed his silver crowns again.

Jason paused and gave Ray more of his boilerplate. "Well, I can't really say at this point. I have to do some research first and see what your neighbors have been selling for."

"To the best of my recollection none of my neighbors have sold lately. I been here some thirty-seven years n'know every one of them." Jason made for his car again as Ray followed. "It's a good neighborhood too, yuh know? Me and my friend Henry Barbour down the way is always doing something for someone round here. We all take care each other round here."

Jason cocked his head toward Ray. "That's not the Henry Barbour that lived down in Ingram some years back?"

"Why yeah, you know old Henry?"

"No, but I think my father did." Jason stopped and pulled his clipboard to his chest. "Did you know a Jimmy Durham?

"Well I'll be damned," Ray said. He looked Jason up and down, and concentrated on his face. "I'll be damned, yeah I knew Jimmy Durham. You kin to him?"

"I'm his youngest son."

"Damned if you ain't! You the spittin image! I knew there was something familiar 'bout you. I'll be damned. He was all right. He n'Sam Smitty would hire us on occasion. Did you know ol' Smitty too? Can't say much for ol' Smitty, but Jimmy, your father, he was always real good to us. Always paid us a fair wage and treated us real good. Yes suh."

"I knew Smitty pretty well. He was around a lot when I was growing up," said Jason, feeling at ease for the first time.

Ray began swaying his tall frame and put a hand to his chin. "I remember one time in particular, your father laughin' at me, just like it was yesterday, him laughin' his head off. I's just'a boy back then, but we was trying to castrate this young calf, n'I was holding the rope round his neck. I's gonna keep him still, yuh see? N'that calf wasn't gonna have no part in being still. He musta gotten wind of what was going on n'got an itch. Your daddy n'Smitty hadn't gotten ready yet n'told me to just hold him until they were ready. Just hold on. Well, I held on all right. That there calf decided it was time to go. Go where I don't know, n'I don't reckon he did either, but he kicked n'heaved, n'I held on, n'I be damned if he didn't throw me ten feet through the air. Old Smitty didn't pay no mind, but your daddy come'a runnin', dusted me off, n'checked my bones. Made sure I was all right. He asked me why I didn't let him go, n'I said to your daddy, 'you told me not to let go.' Your daddy damn near doubled over laughin' n'I can still see him now. Never seen anyone laugh so hard in my life. He laughed. I can still see him laughin' today, I'll tell you. Good Lord. I remember he paid me a call the next day to see if I's really okay. And he payed me a little extra wage that day too. Yes suh, he did."

Jason felt he had just met a small piece of his father he had never known, and he was hungry for more. He found Ray was speaking to him as though he were speaking to an old friend. Ray stared into Jason's smile; into the same smile as Jimmy Durham on the day the reluctant calf decided to skedaddle.

"It was a real shame he died when he did. He had a good heart, but I reckon it wasn't so strong. He was still a young man. Had a lot of good left in him," said Ray.

"I guess he did. I was only thirteen when he died. Old Smitty tried to help us some on the farm, but I guess he didn't do much good. Things kind of fell apart." Jason noticed Ray's flannel shirt stuck above the coat collar the way his father's once did. "I guess we couldn't keep the place up without him."

"My youngest boy you saw in there is thirteen. I'll tell you, it just ain't time to go yet for me. Too much to do. Ain't done with him yet. Gotta keep him on the right path." Ray's eyes panned back to his home. "Gotta keep the place up. Got a daughter I'm trying to get through college. That's what this here loan's for, but I guess they told you that at the bank." Ray paused and turned back to Jason. "Yeah, he died too young. I bet I saw you at the funeral."

"I bet you did," Jason said quietly, his clip board hanging limp in his hand.

"And how are your brothers and sisters?"

"Okay, I guess. We've kind of scattered."

"Scattered, you say? Well, I guess that happens. So, what are you, the third or fourth child?"

"The fourth, and last."

"Well, I had me seven. All raised right here. They all gone now but the youngest. They all turned loose, but they all come back." Ray's big hand reached out and squeezed Jason's forearm and he whispered, "They all miss their momma Nellie, yuh see." He smiled fondly. "They don't care 'bout me none, but they all come back for their momma's cookin'. Yes suh, they always come home."

The first flakes of white began to fall and settle around them. Together they stood in the driveway between the ice-glazed puddles, and Ray shared a few more stories of the old days. Of the time Jimmy Durham's pigs got loose, and of the holiday goose Jimmy would give Ray's family in the good years. As the conversation slowed, but before the onset of any awkwardness, Jason gave his hand once more and he looked Ray in his eyes and told him how nice it was to have met. Of all the times he'd ever said that, Jason knew this was the first time he actually meant it.

Before Jason turned back to his car, he glanced at the warmth spiraling from Ray's chimney and thought he could still smell a hint of Nellie's stew. Ray's quilt of patches and quick fixes seemed to balance and belong, and Jason thought of the underwriting guidelines he would bend and the banking laws he would break to help Ray get his loan.

Jason started the engine and took a sip of cold coffee. Pulling away, he checked the mirror and saw Ray still standing in the driveway, standing like his father stood in his memory, motionless and receding into the distance, alone in a white pearl haze, taking stock of his unfinished estate.

A Story of Hope, Profanity, and Illusion

a triptych in four parts

IN THE SPRING OF 1939, as Mason Remey sank a gold-plated shovel into the ground behind George Washington's home parish, his thoughts were not of his suicide bride but of the inadequacies of the Christian afterlife and his thankful conversion to Baha'i. He was born of higher providence, tracing his line, so he believed, back to Romulus and Remus and the founding of empires. Now he was building his family mausoleum, a two million brick colossus in the Beaux Arts style in which he had been trained in Paris. His wife and a half dozen long-dead ancestors were already slated to be exhumed and reinterred upon completion of the first phase of construction. Another two were pending the outcome of several lawsuits against uncooperative second cousins, all of whom he considered were from inferior branches of the family.

The rector of Pohick Church, who had reluctantly signed off on the Remey land lease, stood by the muddy tree-line as Mason, white-haired and sixty-five, ceremoniously flipped over a shovel of dirt. A photographer from the Washington Times-Herald snapped a picture. The only other witnesses were Mason's secretary and a couple of construction workers perched on bulldozers who had been clearing the site of trees. The building site was surrounded by dense forest – a condition of the land lease as the mausoleum was not to be seen from the historic church or its graveyard. The only reason it was approved was the parish was cash-strapped from nearly ten years of depression.

The rector stepped over the muddy ruts left by the bulldozers. "Mason, are you about done here?" he said. The photographer was already heading up the trail.

"Reverend, you should take note of this day and record your reflections. Your grandchildren may ask you about it."

"We need to talk about your construction schedule. I had to run off a team of your surveyors last Sunday afternoon, right after services. They have no business coming here on Sabbath unless they want to worship."

Mason wrapped the shovel in a cotton towel, being careful not to smear the fresh film of dirt, and handed it to his secretary. He vowed to find a special place for it in the mausoleum. "They were merely trying expedite the very construction you're so keen on finishing."

"Were it up to me, there would be no construction," the rector said. "I don't approve of such personal extravagance when so many good men are out of work."

"I am putting many good men to work," Mason said.

"You're clearing enough land to build a cathedral back here, which wasn't in the lease agreement. And even the cathedral builders rested on Sabbath."

"You've seen the plans," Mason said, pointing out what he considered was obvious. "Most of the mausoleum is to be subterranean."

"Please remember, Mason, this is sacred ground, sacred to both God and country. You're only here because this was approved by the Vestry."

"And your affixed signature."

The rector adjusted his glasses and squinted through the trees toward the cemetery. If any of the grave stones were visible then an injunction might still be possible, but the spring leaves had just unfurled.

Mason was insulted by the reverend's scolding. His mausoleum was no affront to God and country; it was a contribution for which the parish should be grateful. But being honed in diplomacy by both his family and his crusades for Baha'i, he knew how far he could push a man and when he needed to pull back. He also knew well that tragedy can be used for advantage. His wife's suicide had turned into a kind of gift, affording him unearned sympathy and excuses, especially when in need. "I recall your concern over my wife's tragic circumstances, Reverend. I am in debt to you in her memory." His last words were drowned as the men fired up their bulldozers.

"If that's all, Mason, I'll be getting back to my office. Please remember to drop off your construction schedule like you said you would." The rector started up the trail to the church. "You're making an awful lot of racket back here."

∞

A STORY OF HOPE, PROFANITY AND ILLUSION

On Memorial Day, 1974, Gaylord made it as far as the tool shed before the chest pains came on again. His wife's cooking, he assumed, as he chewed a Tums and searched for the grass clippers. He brought the truck around and had to call out three times to his son. "Come'on, Adam! Aunt Jean's waiting on us."

Eleven-year-old Adam gathered the flowers his mother had left bundled on the porch and hopped in the passenger side. He exchanged the flowers for the green stained clippers laying between them on the bench seat. The release popped off and the shears sprang open and flew from his hands.

"Careful with those," his father said, pulling onto the road shaking his head. His son was a curious kid, but aloof, the head-in-the-clouds type. Gaylord wondered if the boy ever heard him.

Adam opened and closed the dull blades. They didn't look like they'd cut anything. "Why doesn't Mom ever come with us?" he asked.

"Your mother doesn't do cemeteries."

They wound a few miles among hills and dairy land before pulling into a gravel drive where a small house sat too close to the road. Aunt Jean came out with her hair tied up, carrying her own flowers like a club. She yanked the door and told Adam to scoot.

"What's got you all knotted up?" Gaylord asked, lighting up a cigarette.

Jean flipped down the visor and flipped it right back up. "You don't have a mirror in this tub?"

"Dad raised us to do without extravagances."

"Dad was a man of the depression. He used to do without soap." Adam's father only grinned. Jean took a moment and continued, "I'm just tired of men that aren't interested in sharing their lives. Al wouldn't budge. Said twice a year is three too many to visit a cemetery."

"We're better off. I'd rather not have Adam riding in the truck bed."

"He knows it means something to me," Jean continued, "but he won't come. He won't stand by me. He's either a coward or a selfish ass."

"We're all those things now and then. I think Al would just rather watch golf."

"Mom doesn't go either," Adam said in his uncle's defense.

"Your mother gets too emotional. It brings her down for the rest of the day and that's no good for anyone."

Jean said, "Your mom doesn't go because she cares too much. Your Uncle Al doesn't go because he doesn't care at all."

They were caught behind two dump trucks loaded with dirt that was spilling onto the pavement and pelting their windshield. The trucks pulled off just before they came to the brick entry gates of the cemetery. Rutted tracks ran into a hollow and separated the field of stones and the old brick church from the forest to the west. Flags planted across the hillside on veterans' graves hung idle on the windless day. Down from where they pulled onto the grass was a cleared field where Gaylord figured he'd be buried one day. Staring across the open grass, he said, "Maybe if you told Al he could bring his 9-iron?"

"I'll tell you what he can do with his 9-iron."

They carried the flowers, twine, and grass clippers up the hill to their family plot, six graves in a row and six more behind them, capped by simple rounded headstones. They hadn't yet looked behind them into the forest where the sound of metal on metal cut the air, and powerful motors revved and idled.

We had never heard of the Baha'i faith or thought much of religion in an organized way. Our Gods were big block V8s, fake IDs, and whatever girl would put out. That night in the Autumn of 1980 our Gods gathered near the driveway of the darkened Rector's house, and the four of us shuffled into the woods in unholy procession, our red-coned flashlights strafing the trees and plastic laced six-packs bouncing off our sides. The leaves felt knee-high as we raked down the trail and shattered the nighttime silence. The abandoned trail arced around the sentinel-like rector's house, which I expected would light up at any second, but only a lone porch light shone by a side door and cast long shadows into the woods.

Dennis said something to Cecilia and grabbed her ass. She squealed. Stuart whispered, "Shut the fuck up," and cut his flashlight.

"The priest's half deaf," Dennis said. "He ain't gonna rouse up nothin."

"Well he's not blind. Shut your light off."

"He's not a priest," Cecilia said. "The sign said Episcopalian. That makes him a preacher or a reverend or something."

After stumbling into a pile of stone columns half covered by honeysuckle, we came to a clearing where a leveled plateau glowed in the half moonlight. An eight-foot wrought iron fence surrounded a ruined courtyard, landscaped with tossed slabs of stone, shattered statuary, and a variety of beer cans. A Mulberry tree had taken root outside the fence, and a knotted rope hung from a branch just beyond the spiked iron bars. Stu and I studied the way over.

"Gimme a boost, Adam," he said. I hoisted him to the first branch, and he scurried up as Cecilia held the flashlight.

After he set himself on the rope, he froze there for a second with his mischievous grin swaying high in the black night sky. That should have been my signal to turn back, but it wasn't worth the abuse. We each scaled the fence and stumbled across the ruin to the edge of the brick courtyard that was sunken a few into the ground. To one side was a higher wall with a massive brick arch flanked by two limestone coat-of-arms. Four-foot slabs of stone had been jammed into the opening, but they didn't quite block the access, leaving a triangle of space to squeeze through.

Stu said, "You go on first, Dennis."

"Fuck that," he said, taking out his stash. He unzipped a plastic sandwich bag and began filling his pipe.

"Courage in a baggie," Stu said. "I'll smoke to that."

And it was courage I was searching for at that point. We had grown up in the country, and a dark night in the forest didn't faze us, but now we were on the threshold of something unknown and perfectly illegal. But we weren't there to grave rob or desecrate the place. We couldn't have if we tried. The Pagans were said to have wrecked it over the years, and they had done a fine job. It was known simply as "The Crypts," and its exploration was a rite-of-passage for any high-schooler in the county. My sense of the place at the time was that it dated back to the Civil War, and though I did not believe in haunting, the place felt haunted and filled with sadness. I imagined it a rich burial place for front line generals or forgotten heroes whose lace draped mothers had sent to battle, never to see them return. I remember years ago my father and my Aunt Jean mentioning something about the crypts in passing when we were visiting the nearby cemetery, the cemetery where he is now buried, but I don't recall the conversation.

Mason wanted to inspect the Remeum one last time before leaving for his new home in Haifa, in the newly formed country of Israel. There had been some mischief during the eleven years of construction, including several attempted break-ins, but there was no significant damage. Mason's foreman guided him through the entry garden to the door of the outdoor atrium, which was ringed with hand carved bas-reliefs of the seminal events in American history, of which Mason's family had taken part. His father was a distinguished rear admiral, and other ancestors included a pilgrim on the Mayflower and a vestryman at this very church. The foreman showed him the crowbar damage at the door lock and hinges.

"This time they gave up and scaled the wall. They got to the main door," the foreman said. Mason carried a roll of architectural plans as he was led through the columned atrium to the brick arched door of the narthex. This door to the underground chambers was damaged in the same way.

"Superficial," Mason said, examining the hinges. He admired the two stone lions flanking the entrance, carved by the same artist who had sculpted the Iwo Jima Memorial. "They did not gain entry. These two beasts did their job."

For a man of seventy-six, Mason swung open the heavy wooden doors with ease and passed under the arch. Stepping down into the first chamber, he paused to admire the statue of his beloved parents, the admiral in full regalia and his wife bunched up in a Victorian bustle. He was sure if his father had lived long enough and seen Mason's growing influence in Baha'i that he would have learned to approve. But thanks to his brother's stubborn refusal to have them reinterred, his parents were still buried in Arlington under a simple granite cenotaph, lost among the hordes of forgotten citizen soldiers. Hardly a place for a family of such prominence. His great-grandfather, George Mason, should also have been in the Remium, but the proprietors of Gunston Hall were not amused at Mason's request, and now spoke to him only through their attorneys.

Though he always stopped before his parent's statue and said a prayer to Baha'i'abdul, he passed by his late wife's chapel without a glance, as he did each time he came. He didn't kneel or offer a prayer, even at her reinterment. Seeing his own empty sarcophagus did not bother him, as he instructed that his name be carved into the stone only after his passing. Due to an oversight, his birth year had already been engraved: 1874 - 19__. He scoffed at the sight of it as if scoffing the idea of death itself.

Down a short corridor adorned with mosaics of glass and stone, he stood under the grand design, the Baha'i House of Worship he would construct. On an open pedestal meant to one day hold a burial vault, Mason rolled out his new plans for what was to rise above him. The six story temple came to him in a prophetic vision, as did his destined place within the faith, all of which further justified the Remeum against his critics. He knew he would one day lay here under its dome.

"Mr. Remey!" a voice called down the corridor. Footsteps followed, and Mason turned to see the new rector coming toward him. He quickly rolled up the plans. "Mr. Remey, we need to talk."

"Of course, Reverend. What can I do for you?"

"Rumor has it you're leaving the country. Moving to Palestine, of all places."

"Shoghi Effendi has called me there in his service."

"Well, I'm not greatly impressed by all this Baha'i business, but that's not my concern. You have some obvious vandalism issues and I'm concerned about it spilling over into the churchyard."

"Construction sites are magnets for theft and vandalism. As soon as we complete this phase, I'm sure things will calm down."

"And what of this second phase we keep hearing about? It's been referred to time-and-time again, but the Vestry still hasn't seen the plans."

"I assure you, upon securing funding, the next phase will be presented for your approval. As you know, it's still in the planning phase, so there's nothing yet to show you."

The rector eyed the roll of blueprints. "How can it be that this isn't big enough?" he asked, aided by his outstretched hands. "I've never seen a family crypt as vast as what you've built here."

"Family and friends, Reverend. I have a large number of each, patiently waiting a resting place in the Remeum. As to your concerns over vandalism, I will see about heavier doors. The iron gates are still being fabricated, but should be installed this summer. It will be a fortress."

∞

Gaylord was winded from climbing the hill and paused there to rub his chest and light a cigarette. He watched Jean and Adam breaking down the bunches of flowers to make arrangements for each grave. The boy was into arts and crafts, but Gaylord didn't even know the difference between arts and crafts. He'd taken him deer hunting a few years back, but it was easy to see it wasn't in Adam's constitution. He didn't mind that so much, but he worried about him. He just wanted to toughen him up a bit. Gaylord dropped to his knees and went to work with the clippers, dressing down the skirt of spring grasses around his parent's headstone. The grounds-keeper did little more than mow between the stones, but he didn't mind that either. This was his way to pay homage and perhaps to instill a sense of responsibility in his son.

Aunt Jean had a system where the ancestors she did not know received simple uniform arrangements, which formed a base-line for the ones she did know. In this way her parents always received the largest tribute, which included red roses and hyacinth, the favored flowers of the family. A beloved uncle was also well planted, whereas a cousin who had tormented her in childhood, later to die in a car accident, received only a handful of forsythia.

Adam counted out the bouquets. "You're missing one," he said.

"No, I am not," Jean replied, going about her work. Gaylord glanced up to monitor his sister. They'd been through this before. He finished his parent's row, which included Gaylord and Jean's brother, and watched as Adam and his sister began placing the flowers. As he suspected, Jean skipped their brother's grave.

"Are we going to get into this again?" Gaylord said.

"You know how I feel."

"You ever think this was the kind of treatment that was so hard on him in the first place?"

Jean wouldn't rise from her work, trying to make leaning flowers stand. "I only know what he did, and to hell with him for doing it."

"I though he died in a car wreck," Adam said.

Jean pointed at her brother's grave. "He died in a car all right. And he was a wreck."

"You've said enough, Jean."

"The boy's old enough to handle it. Adam, your Uncle Henry ran a hose from the exhaust into the car and gassed himself to death. In my book that disqualifies him from receiving flowers."

Adam stared at his uncle's grave with different eyes, more alert now and less trusting, as if wondering if his uncle was buried there at all.

"Well someone planted a flag on him," Gaylord pointed out. "You want to deny him that too?"

"I suppose he earned that," Jean said in a lone breath of empathy.

"Do you remember much about him, Adam?" It was suddenly important to Gaylord that his son remember his brother. "You were only six or so when he died."

"I remember him," Adam said. "He showed me his war medals once."

"You see, Jean? He carried that war around every day." He said to his son, "Uncle Henry saw the worst of it, including hand-to-hand combat at Mortain and the liberation of one of those camps. He was not the same man when he came home."

"That's not an excuse. He had years to get his life straightened out," Jean argued. "Now clip those stones so I can finish planting these."

"You are a hard woman." Gaylord settled to his knees before the second row of graves. When they finished, as Jean was bumming a cigarette off her brother, they were both distracted by a loud crash from the forest behind them. Adam was onto the third headstone by the time they noticed what he was doing.

"What are you up to, young man?" Jean asked. Adam didn't stop until he'd collected one flower from each of the eleven graves. He used twine to bind the awkward arrangement and placed it over his dead uncle. Then he stared at his aunt and waited.

∞

We sat on the sloping stones in front of the arch, and Dennis passed around the pipe, first to Cecilia who giggled through a few tokes, then to Stu who held his breath like a free-diver. As I took my turn, Stu crouched and explored the hole with his flashlight, then shimmied feet first under the arch. I went in after him and we found ourselves perched on the spring line about ten feet above the floor. The passage had been filled with a layer of brick and broken out again. Below us a shattered wood door frame had been fashioned into a poor man's ladder, with several crooked boards nailed down its height. We each hopped off the last rung like Neil Armstrong and landed in a sea of aluminum cans, which was not at all like Neil Armstrong.

"Good God, almighty," Stu said, laughing and flashing his light around. We were in an entry vestibule, and in front of us was another high archway and steps down into larger room. We got Dennis and Cecilia off the ladder and kicked our way into the first chamber. Cecilia screamed as one of our lights caught a vandalized statue on the central pedestal – a headless man in uniform with a row of medals across his chest and, who I would assume to be, his kneeling wife. In her hand was a leftover roach, and someone had used wax and lipstick to make her face into a mask grotesque. Red candles had burned on her husband's vacant neck and left streaks of wax blood running down his body. Someone had blackened his crotch with a lighter.

"Holy Fuck," Dennis said. The room was one large brick barrel vault resting on squat heavy columns on either side of the room. Between each column were pedestals and the hammered remains of statuary, torsos of wingless angels and nameless saints, their ruined extremities tossed about the chamber with ankle-high beer cans and whiskey bottles. It was hard to tell what the floor was made of. I bent down and sifted through the debris. It had flooded before and was covered by ash-like dirt, splinters of wood, square chips of glass, and tiny white sticks like driftwood. Many of the cans were rusty, made long before the switch to aluminum. The room had a great weight to it, a weight of time and earth and root. For just a few seconds we all turned off our flashlights and felt the blackness known only to the dead.

I went into the next chamber where an enormous stone sarcophagus filled the room. It was embellished with deep engraved columns, arches and hand-carved scalloping, reminding me of something from the Crusades. Its massive stone top, alone weighing several tons, was raised on wood blocks so one could peek inside. On one end was engraved "1874 - 19__." Unless he was 106 years old, the intended inhabitant had never moved in, and I wondered what had become of him. Given its size, I thought the stone must have been carved in-place and the crypts built around it. Four corridors sprouted off from this tomb and made it the God center of the complex.

I heard a couple of crashes. Screams and hoots echoed from the first room, and flashlights parried about. Dennis and Cecilia came in behind me. "We've got company," he said, leading her by the hand deeper into the complex. Dennis had been there before and told me his ambition was to fuck Cecilia in one of the empty tombs. I followed them to the end of the main corridor that was barricaded by a wall of plain cinder block. God knows how far back it once went. Two quick lefts put us in a room that double-backed from the direction we came. In the center was an unadorned and uncapped burial vault.

Dennis lit his pipe again, handed it to me, and nosed up to the vault to look inside. He hopped onto the edge and extended a hand to Cecilia. Once she was inside, he said to me, "Don't smoke it all," and tossed me the baggie. That was my signal to get out, and also an untold yet understood signal to try and keep everyone the hell out of that room.

I went back to the anteroom and lit up. I lit up a long one and breathed in deep to forget how alone I felt. Tooling around an abandoned crypt sounded like a good idea at first, but being there was a mixture of sadness, regret, and the sublime feeling that I'd been there before. For all their former grandeur, the tombs had been forgotten, and all those buried were lost. And there I was loitering among this staggering loss of memory, smoking dope by a cinder block wall while my friend got laid. It all drove home the fact that I myself was lost. Things weren't good at home. My father was dead two years going, and my mother wasn't the same. I wasn't feeling much in life to be excited about.

The carryin' on from the new band of partiers was getting louder, and I heard Stu making nice with them. Flashlights shone down the main corridor and lit the cinder block wall beside me. Then a big burley son-of-a-bitch came around the corner and blinded me.

"What the fuck you doing in my crypt?" he said.

∞

Mason Remey sat among stacks of files and rolls of building plans in his study on Mass Avenue in Kalorama. He had returned from Haifa two years ago, in 1960, to organize support of the American branch of Baha'i, convinced of his rightful ascension to Second Guardian of the faith. Mason was not a man who trusted the wisdom of committees. Left without a true Guardian, he reasoned, the followers of Baha'i'abdul would splinter apart, drift aimlessly, and eventually disband. The First Guardian had not chosen a successor, but had named Mason President of the International Baha'i Council. And many years ago, Abdu'l

Baha himself, before his own passing, had often referred to Mason as his "son." That, combined with a prophetic vision, was enough for Mason to take up the burden to carry the faith, but the thanks he received was scorn and outrage. He was attacked as senile and an egomaniac, and compared to the whore of Babylon. The Baha'i Council declared him a covenant breaker and promptly excommunicated him. And he, in turn, excommunicated them.

His assistant, Pepe, came running up the staircase. He was born in New Jersey, but had enough residual Italian accent to be charming. He was a faithful servant.

"Mr. Remey," he said, pausing to catch his breath, "the vestry is going forward with a new lawsuit."

Mason was not impressed. "They already have their injunction. Beyond that, there won't be funds available to complete the temple in my lifetime."

"It's not just about stopping the temple. They're suing for outright possession. They want to break the lease and take ownership of the Remeum."

"Mason lifted his cane, fiddled with it for a moment and slammed it on the drafting table. "They will not take my Pantheon. It is already home to fifteen of my family and friends. Fifteen interments! How does one seize the graves of another?"

"They have had enough of the vandalism."

"The vandalism happened on their watch! They actually encouraged it, so as to help their case against the temple. My only mistake was not being here to personally guard its sanctity."

"The temple, Mason. The *Baha'i* temple," Pepe said. "It is simple bigotry. They are paranoid of what they don't understand."

Mason gazed out the window up the street at the South Korean Embassy. He lived in the heart of Embassy Row, with ambassadors and dignitaries for neighbors. Now he had to deal with the whims of rural vestrymen in a backwater parish. "They will not break the lease," he declared. "We can repair the Remeum and make it secure. The plans for the temple I'll leave to the New Baha'i under the Hereditary Guardianship. One day they'll construct it in my absence . . . once funds are available."

"In the meantime, I will contact your attorney," Pepe said. "The parish is said to be drawing up papers this week."

Mason shrugged. "I know most of the judges personally."

"Two of their vestrymen are judges."

"What court, small claims? I've dined with Supreme Court Justices. My late wife and I threw a party in this very house for Vice-President Curtis."

"That was over twenty years ago, Mr. Remey."

Mason rested the tip of his cane on the floor and balanced it under his palm. Despite his age, he could not quite believe he needed the assistance of a cane. "And they said they wanted to negotiate. They were sure we could come to an understanding. Liars and blasphemers. There has never been a day I regretted leaving such a small-minded institution."

Pepe turned to leave, but Mason called him back.

"Pepe, please . . . come to me." Mason motioned for him to come closer and placed his cold hand on the young man's forehead. "Thank you, Pepe. Thank you. You understand me," he said, slipping his hand to the younger man's cheek. "You are like a son to me." His assistant accepted the compliment, though awkwardly as he rearranged his hands. Mason grasped Pepe's neck and continued with a warbling voice that exposed his age. "Did I ever tell you I designed Baha'i Houses of Worship for Haifa and Tehran, the plans for the Persian temple blessed by

Abdu'l Baha himself? They will both be built. Once I am vindicated and recognized as the Second Guardian, they will be built as well."

"I'm sure they will," Pepe said, slipping out of Mason's reach. "I will contact your attorney." He left the old man alone with his plans.

Mason hung his cane on the edge of the drafting table and began a preliminary sketch of a small vessel, a reliquary, to hold a lock of his hair. Or perhaps a finger, of which he had ten. These fingers had designed two of the very temples in which the followers of Baha'i worship daily. He playfully toyed with the idea of which House of Worship would receive which finger, then he unfurled a roll of blueprints to admire the cut-away section of the American Temple rising to the kingdom of God, his Remeum as its foundation and his own tomb at its sacred heart.

"Let them sue," he said.

∞

Jean was used to fighting men her own age, but not a boy of eleven. Adam stood there defying her, his face turning red as he waited for her reaction. "You messed up all my arrangements," she said, with less rancor than usual.

"They're not your flowers," Adam shot back. "Those are the ones my mom gave us."

"Well that's my ball of twine."

Adam grabbed the flowers, slid off the binding and threw it at her.

"Now that's enough," Gaylord said, pinching out his cigarette. "You don't act that way."

That voice from Gaylord was all it took to cut the boy's attitude. Adam apologized, but clearly didn't mean it, then sulked down the line of graves to read the stones. Gaylord had noticed his son's change when Jean mentioned Henry's suicide. He was right, Adam wasn't ready for that.

"That's an emotional boy you got there," Jean said, as if implying a character flaw.

"You insinuating something?"

"He's sure as hell our blood."

Gaylord tapped another cigarette from his pack. "I suppose he can get emotional about some things. That doesn't mean he's like Henry."

Jean treaded down the hill toward the truck. "I was going to say he was like me."

∞

I offered him my pipe.

"Fuck yeah," the brute said, taking a whiff of the bowl. "You're all right." Dennis always got the good stuff. I didn't know what the good stuff was, just that it worked well in the lungs and making friends. My new friend wore studded leather and the widest beard I'd ever seen, sticking far beyond his ears while his hair was combed back in a long pony-tail. His pock-marked face reminded me more of cigarette burns than the scars of acne, and I watched it turn varying shades of purple as he held his breath.

"Ahhhhh," he went, releasing an enormous cloud of smoke. "That's the fifth variety of cannabis I've sampled today." His eyes glowed white in the darkness and gave him the appearance of a madman. There was some shuffling around behind me, and he looked over my shoulder.

"My buddy and his girl are in there," I said. He was more interested in the herb, so I gave him the whole bag.

He took me by the arm. "Say no more." I couldn't believe he squeezed through that hole under the arch.

His gang was coming up the main hall – I counted seven, eight, nine of them. We were way outnumbered. These weren't people to mess with. When we had the crypts to ourselves there was something sad yet holy about the place, unlike anything I've felt before, and I could justify my presence as an explorer of ancient ruins, an amateur historian, or benevolent spirit of the curious. But with the arrival of this gang of burn-outs our presence quickly devolved into desecration, and the idea of desecration offended me. Though I was indifferent about coming here, now I was ashamed.

"My name's Del" he said, pinching my arm and admiring his new stash.

His last buddy who came staggering down the hall said, "Stands for Delirious."

Delirious's friend was far down the drug chain, obviously having gone beyond a few beers and loosely rolled joints. His name was Ray Dude. I don't remember how I learned his name, but the name itself is etched in my mind, likely because it rhymes with quaalude. His eyes echoed his name and looked somewhere else entirely as he brought up the rear of the stumbling chain of losers. We all filed into the room opposite where Dennis and Cecilia were fucking. All the women among them had hair that appeared never to have been brushed, the last of whom was being closely followed by Stu, who was pawing at the hem of her coat. He called her Maggie.

Del pushed me in after them. The room was another heavy brick barrel vault where all the debris had been swept to the perimeter. Everyone sat on the dirt floor in a circle around a make-shift altar of half burnt candles. It was damp, but not muddy. Everything down there was damp. One of the guys pulled a bong out of his coat, while his girlfriend opened a Sucrets tin filled with different colored pills and started counting out prescriptions for each of her friends.

Stu was working on Maggie and trying to be funny. He said, "So, you come here often?"

"Shit," Del chimed in from across the circle, "I been coming here ten years."

Ray Dude said, "shit," and nodded.

"My older cousin was fucking around here back in the sixties. Said they used to set off fucking bombs farther back before they closed that section off. He was the first one to dig back in after they tried to bury the place in the early seventies." Del stared into the orange lit embers at the tip of the bong stem as he pulled a can of Pabst from his coat. "He got too old for that shit now."

This was when I noticed the girl next to me gently swaying side-to-side. Her face was long and plain, her lips parted and chapped. Her eyes were open one minute and closed the next, which seemed to give me permission to look over her body. Her coat splayed out at her belly, shaped like a church bell. She kept swaying from side-to-side and I expected soft sounds to come from her, a brief poem or a chant.

"Cindy's my love monkey," Del said, sitting on my opposite side, "carrying my love monkey child."

I was suddenly made to feel more uncomfortable than I already was for sitting between a man named Delirious and his pregnant love monkey. I offered to switch places, but Del pushed my shoulder down.

"Sit down. It's not like she's my wife," he said, thinking that was pretty funny. Cindy kept swaying as the bong made its round. A pill from Sucrets Girl's tin made its way to her, and she opened her eyes to acknowledge it before setting it on her tongue and closing her chapped lips. She took nothing to wash it down.

As the room filled with smoke, I heard a noise from the other chamber and another in rhythm, and I knew it was Dennis and Cecilia. Stu got a big grin on his face and put his hand on Maggie's tit. Some of the guys started cracking up and coughing smoke, and so did Maggie. Ray Dude went to a corner to take a piss and as he turned to zip up, I noticed something in the darkness behind him. My flashlight lit a cracked stone urn that had taken Ray Dude's bitter donation, engraved delicately with: "The Ashes Charles Estherbrook."

∞

Mason sat in his garden high above Florence. In front of him was an espresso and a folded Herald Tribune, which he no longer read. At ninety-four his vision was failing, but under a large round magnifying glass was an open book on the prophecies of world cataclysm. Pepe, now his adopted son and power-of-attorney, was sitting by the tall windows at a desk shuffling papers. He had just gotten off the phone and appeared bothered by the call. He brought a folder to the table and sat down.

"Mason," he said, removing his glasses. "Papa, the court has decided. The Remeum will be handed over to the church in five years." He waited for a response, but Mason was silent. Pepe removed some papers from the envelope and laid one before him. "I have drafted a letter to the parish informing them you have received the court order and will be making arrangements to move your remaining relatives to a safe burial place. Your brother-in-law is also working on it locally. He once spoke of a cemetery in New York as a possibility. Do you remember?"

"Do you remember" was all Mason heard. At ninety-four his memory, in agreement with his vision, was no longer clear and often selective. But his grandest moments were still vivid, if not embellished, as he had replayed them so many times – the flashes of light and enlightenment from turn-of-the-century Paris apartments and Tehran coffee houses, the Baha'i Houses of Worship he built in Australia and Uganda, and the blessed Abdu'l Baha calling him 'my son.' And he could recall all of the milestones of the Remeum: the installation of the Bruge Madonna and the bas relief of the USS Yorktown, the removal of the centering from the grand entry arch, and the arrival and placing of his own sarcophagus, hand-carved by artisans in Lisbon.

But the one memory he tried to forget but could not was the interment of his wife. He married late-in-life and considered Gertrude the last best chance for offspring, perhaps providing a son who would be a significant figure in the faith. Years later, when convinced of his eventual ascension to head the fledgling religion, he realized that when his wife killed herself she also murdered Baha'i's future Third Guardian.

Pepe tried again to get his attention. "Mason," he said, spreading out the photos of the vandalism – open tombs of lost relatives, splintered caskets, empty urns of old friends.

He did not need to see these again, the evidence of the pagans ransacking the temple. Those interred had been blessed and were now just ashes and bones. What is permanent are the words. Mason's journals and writings, including personal letters from Abdu'l Baha, had already been handed over to the archivist at Cornell, his alma mater, releasing him from concern that his influence might wane. They would be transferred to his temple in General Washington's parish once Baha'i gains prominence, realizes its mistake, and rights this terrible wrong. The temple will be constructed in its rightful place, and his sacred bodily remains will be entombed in the sarcophagus beneath the altar floor. He was never more sure of it. And he was never more sure that his father would have been proud. His fall and rise were destined to solidify his place in Baha'i mythology. So the temple of Jerusalem had fallen, Mason pondered, so must the Remeum to insure it's resurrection.

He took up the pen and shook his signature onto the page. "Get them out," he said. "Get them all out. I don't care what you do with them."

∞

Descending the hill toward the truck, Aunt Jean caught sight of a slim square headstone that seemed out-of-place among the more traditional monuments. Its fresh grave had sunk and more dirt had recently been raked over and feathered into the grasses. "I heard that nut finally died," she said, reading the inscription.

"What nut?"

"Remey. That nut you worked for after the war, building that temple to himself. Newspaper said he just missed a hundred." She motioned toward the deeps woods to the west where machines were roaring, and metal clanged on metal. "Sounds like he's still working on it."

Adam's father regarded the fresh grave. The inscription read:

IN
AFFECTIONATE MEMORY
OF
MY WIFE
GERTRUDE HEIM REMEY
MDCCCLXXXVIII - MCMXXXII
OUR MARRIAGE SOLEMNIZED IN
THE PRO CATHEDRAL CHURCH
OF
THE HOLY TRINITY
PARIS FRANCE, SEPTEMBER 11, 1931

The script ran into the grass and down into the earth, and looked like it could have gone on for a few paragraphs. Jean counted on her fingers, trying to decipher the roman numerals.

"They moved her again," Gaylord said, shaking his head. He motioned toward the woods beyond the graveyard that screened the Remeum. "The first time they moved her back there. I think this is the same stone that was mounted by her tomb." He knew she'd shot herself in the head in their home in Kalorama, but he didn't want to say anything in front of Adam, who was meandering down the hill, reading names and dates. "She's not going to get any peace with all this moving around."

Right when Adam was within earshot, Jean said, "Wasn't she a suicide too?"

Gaylord didn't know what to do with his sister. "Just a year after they married," he said, shaking his head. "Her tomb back there was capped with a life-size carving of her holding a baby. I figure that's why Remey built the place. Couldn't handle the loss." That stopped the conversation for a moment as they stood there on the side of the hill staring into the woods, listening to another pair of dump trucks grinding their gears on the way to the old mausoleum. "I don't hold anything against Remey. My first job was carrying bricks for him."

"Yeah," Jean said, "He must have been a real prince. They should have buried his wife next to Henry."

"Who should be?" Adam asked, joining them.

"This poor woman who married a lunatic."

"This poor woman?" Gaylord said, raising his voice. "What makes her so innocent and Henry so guilty?"

Jean looked off balance on the hill and shifted her hips. "I'm just saying he must have had something to do with it."

"She killed herself too?" Adam asked, staring in disbelief.

Gaylord laid into his sister. "So being married to a rich eccentric is excuse enough to blow your brains out, but the goddamned German army trying to kill you for eight months straight doesn't count?"

Jean closed her eyes. She blew smoke out her nose and wiped it, then pulled it together. "That's not what I meant."

Adam marched to a nearby grave capped with an American flag and an enormous floral arrangement. He came back with a single orange lily and placed it in front of Mrs. Remey's headstone. Then he headed for the truck.

"I'm sorry, Gaylord," Jean said.

"He was my brother."

"He was my brother too."

"We could have helped him. It was our job to help him."

Jean wouldn't face him. "I suppose it was."

Gaylord felt something pass between them, he and his sister, whom he rarely understood. His anger waning, he turned to watch Adam who was below them now, nearing the forest.

"And he is my son."

∞

It was a room without memory, forlorn and buried, and though it tried to speak to me I couldn't make out its words. And so from a place of resignation, I submitted to the strange fraternity of wanderers encircled around the altar of burning wax. Three repetitive cries echoed from the depths of the crypt, and again silence. Everyone's movements seemed to slow down, but we knew it was not ourselves slowing but time playing tricks as time does in dark chambers of shattered art and scattered bone. The girl next to me stopped swaying, which had a profound effect on the smoke filled room. Her swaying had set the pace of activity: the passing of pills, the filling of pipes, and the squeezing of tits. I felt time slow again as she removed something from her pocket and held it under her palm. At first I thought it was a comb or maybe a joint. Then in a swift and surprisingly graceful maneuver, she let the switch blade spring free and ran its edge diagonally across her wrist. It was so smooth that no one said a word. I watched the skin separate and the black ooze out of her. Blood wasn't red in the dimness of the crypts and only when it pulsed with her heart did someone shine a light directly on the flow. Then time was moving very quickly.

The drunk and stoned ghosts of ourselves swirled around the room, everyone flying in different directions, though there was only one way out. Sucrets Girl screamed and dropped her array of pills into the piss-soaked ash, while her boyfriend grabbed his bong from some guy in mid-toke and shook out the water. Screams and panicked cries co-mingled with the groans and grunts of the ecstasy of Cecilia.

"Oh fuck me!" Del screamed, throwing me aside. He lunged toward this girl he did not claim, grabbing her arm and squeezing with both hands, but it was like wringing out a wet dishtowel, her dark blood dripping through his fingers under wavering flashlights. "What the fuck did you do?" Maggie crawled over unwinding her scarf as Ray Dude tripped over her trying to get out. "Oh fuck," Del said, over and over. He released her arms and stared at his hands in disbelief. "Oh fuck." Cindy gave Del an accusatory glare, as if saying, "look what you did to me." He crawled into a corner and began punching a vacant stone pedestal. He punched solid stone and said his words over and over.

Stu grabbed my coat and tugged. "We gotta get the fuck out of here," he said. Then he was gone. Why I didn't run too, I don't know. Here was this girl I did not know who had decided to end her life. This was none of my business.

Maggie wrapped her old wool scarf around Cindy's wrist, which didn't do a thing. The one guy who hadn't run stripped off his coat, ripped his shirt into pieces and made a couple of tourniquets. He tightened the first one so hard it tore and the pent up surge of blood shot across the room and splattered Delirious across the back. The second one held. I gave them my sweat-shirt and we used Cindy's bloody switch blade to slice it into bandages, wrapping them directly on the open wound. All along the girl was calm and once again swaying, submitting to the ages, smiling as if satisfied that the father of her child was destroying his hands on a piece of fine Italian marble and losing his mind.

There were only three of us left to get her out of there: me, Maggie and Tourniquet Guy, who was having a hard time just standing up. He was too thin, and stringy in hair, bone and intellect, likely emaciated by years of casual drugs and inactivity. It disturbed me when I realized he reminded me of myself, or at least what I feared I might resemble in another few years. We got under each arm and walked Cindy out of the room as far as the main corridor where she collapsed. Her pregnancy made her center-of-gravity low, like the great weight of an iron church bell pulling us both to the floor. I watched as her eyes rolled back into her head. The weight of the brick barrel vaults also seemed to rest on our shoulders. We somehow got her up again, this time dragging her a few yards at a time and resting. Maggie held the flashlight as our own stuck out our back pockets and jostled over the ceiling as we kicked through the debris.

We finally got back to the entry and found Stu cussing under the arch.

"That Ray Dude asshole broke the ladder on the way out."

Calling it a ladder was being generous. The long section of board had split length-wise and was lying to one side, its steps hanging useless by one nail each. I grasped better now how we had come in. The arch was eight feet wide and a dozen or so feet to the top where a triangle of dim blueish light was seeping into the hall. The whole opening had been bricked in, but several man-size holes had been punched through and patched over and over again. On the inside were the bent remains of an ornamental iron gate still mortared in-place. It had taken great and repeated determination to break in there over the years. The iron gate was mostly intact under the side of the arch that was open. I knew I could climb up and shimmy back out, but not while carrying another human being.

Cindy was out cold, which could have been from either the loss of blood, the drugs, or both. We sat her against the wall, and Maggie pinched her cheek and spoke into her ear. I tried to catch my breath and stared into the girl's face. All the peacefulness of her swaying had given way to a deathly pallor. The spirit she had about her had fled, leaving nothing in its wake but the overwhelming shadow of finality. It was then I felt my fear begin to weaken me physically. My body shivered. I begged Stu to get on his hands and knees.

"Fuck that," he said.

"We got to get her the fuck outta here!"

"You get down in that shit."

Tourniquet Man came over and dropped onto the floor amidst the garbage. Stu yelled, "topside," so I got on the guy's back and steadied myself, while Stu climbed the iron gate and worked his way onto my shoulders. He was light, but now seemed to weigh a ton. I was exhausted. Stu's head was over the gate and just under the opening, but there was no one left to hoist the girl up. Maggie shone the light on us. "This is not going to work," she said, as if speaking to idiots. She couldn't even stand her friend up.

"We either gotta pull Dennis out of Cecilia, or get that big moose back there to help," Stu said, climbing down. I was about to go after Dennis when I stopped cold. To wade through all the trash and debris unheard was not possible, but there he stood, Del, and we had not heard him. His hands hung to his knees and resembled clubs, his fingers and knuckles congealed into dripping stumps. In self-revulsion, he held them away from his sides. He was the only one big enough to carry the girl by himself, and as he considered the four of us he must have realized that. The first thing he did was hoist Maggie up top. Then Del picked up the future mother of his child from her armpits and backed into place.

"Get on the fucking floor," he said, and this time Stu didn't argue. He and Tourniquet Man got on their hands and knees, side-by-side, and braced themselves. Del kneeled and told me to get on. I climbed onto his shoulders and balanced there. Then in an amazing feat of drug-induced strength, Del rose with the weight of me and the girl, and back-stepped onto the two straining men. I felt Maggie's feet settle onto my shoulders.

And so I found myself in a human chain of flesh among crushed metal and broken glass, my thigh on a stranger's shoulder, a muddy sneaker by my ear. I could see into the grand chamber the silhouette of the headless man in uniform and his demon wife looking on our folly with approval. Together our band of misfits raised the girl and unborn child, Del the father passing her limp body into my arms. She was heavier than I imagined. I am not a strong man. Taking care around the tourniquets, I strained to lift her pale arms of loose cold flesh, then shifted under her pelvic bone palming the womb, stretched warm and tight. We paused there to reset, and in the casket-like air I felt a sudden chill of a pre-winter wind rush down from the triangle of sky above. It was then my father came back to me. I gave girl the slightest squeeze, a prayer for the dead, and hoisted her under the archway.

Modern Predators

WE CRUISED THE AVENUES of the Embassy District to the beat of the street lights as I silently rehearsed my lines. Adriane parted her lips, pulled down the visor, and raised her chin to the mirror to apply more blush – for the third time. She was in a fluster I hadn't seen on our first two dates and was beginning to make me anxious.

"Just be a gentleman, Lee," she said, preening herself in the mirror. "And don't talk too much. You'll be fine."

"I think I can handle myself, Adriane."

She checked her hair for bounce and flipped up the visor. Then realizing her offence, she reached over pressed a hand to my leg.

"This is a real opportunity for you," she said, though her spirit quickly soured as her eyes swept across the interior of my car. Before I could comment, she lunged for my coat sleeve.

"Here, right here!"

It wasn't as though I could have missed the entry gate –
it was as big as my house. Beyond the gate the ambassador's
residence was lit up as if ready for a night launch, a spectacle
that made any passerby want to run home and bring back the
kids. We rumbled over the cobblestone drive to the front
portico where a white gloved valet showed us his teeth and
opened Adriane's door. The parking attendant came to my
side and extended a hand for the keys.

"Your party, sir?" he asked.

"Constance and Miller."

He avoided eye contact and slid into my twelve-year-old
Toyota. I stood under the brilliance and watched him drive
the wretched car into the motor court, sliding it between a
Mercedes and a Volvo. He had to have had a smirk on his
face. I imagined him in the morning scrubbing the inevitable
oil stain off the stone pavers, and took comfort in the
thought.

"Are you coming?" Adriane was scolding and outwardly
nervous, which made no sense to me. I was the one living
outside the Beltway with a starving architectural practice, and
more than a little desperate for new work. All week I had
churned this evening over in my head, obsessing over the
possibilities, but Adriane already knew the scene. Now a
trusted member of the DC press corp, she had earned a
place on the "A" list for State Dinners.

The hand-cut glass in the front windows glittered and
winked as if the joke were on me. I straightened my neck tie,
painfully aware it was the wrong type, and took Adriane's
hand as we climbed the steps of the portico under the lights.
On crossing the threshold the rush of servants continued as
the maître d' relieved us of our coats. Now I was exposed,
tuxedo-less, and shaded with the fear that the make and year
of my car would be made public.

Ushered through the grand foyer, which looked like it had been carved from a single block of marble, we were received in the adjacent salon to the sound of chatter and a Mozart divertimento. Someone tapped silver on crystal, and all eyes turned to us.

"Ladies and Gentleman. Miss. Adriane Constance and Mr. Leland Miller."

Mozart played his notes, but the joy was filtered with indifference. It was as though we had just been given an award of great effect that we had not earned, and were now forced to explain ourselves to a confounded audience.

We were examined for an awkward moment like new Christmas ornaments before Adriane broke the prism by waving to a colleague, Lexie, who writes for one of the local political rags. She scooted toward her through the crowd, and I sauntered behind as though I belonged. The salon recovered from our interruption and a waiter intercepted us. I ordered a Stolichanaya – double, and Adriane a Chardonnay. The drinks appeared in our hands.

Adriane gave Lexie a mock hug, being careful not to ruffle her dress, which poured like a waterfall of lace over her impregnated belly. On Lexie's arm was the father, though he could have been *her* father.

"You must be Lee," she said approvingly. "Adriane told me you have your own practice." Lexie came to my side, exchanging her husband's arm for mine. "Let me point out who's who. You never know where your next commission might come from." She began by introducing me to her ancient spouse, whose name I immediately forgot. Then she nodded around the room, marking every CEO, diplomat, and Congressman. After this covert introduction, she made a common remark about the weather, then dropped my arm and spilled into shop-talk conversation with Adriane. The silver-haired husband stood by his trophy, scanning the room and being immaculate. We glanced at one another as if we were sharing an elevator.

Having no idea how to engage the crowd, I employed the architect's natural defense and began examining the room I was standing in. It was hard to discern where the wall stopped and the ceiling began, as the seam flowed with gold-leaf and tracery. The silk paneled walls looked like they had been stretched and tested with a thrown quarter. As I soaked in the opulence and tried to get comfortable, an old woman in blue sequins took a sudden interest in me.

"I remember you. I know we've met." False revelation shone in her eyes. "The Phillip's Collection Gala!" She began sputtering something about the DuPonts. I had never seen her before in my life, but I decided it was nice to see her again, and we started reliving old times. My every word was golden. She motioned to her husband.

"Howard, dear, this is Mr. Miller. Mr. Miller is an ar-chi-tect."

Had she spoken the word with more pretension, the house might have thrown open its windows and belched us onto the lawn. My new friend, Howard, ambled over with a whisky in his grip. His face was parched like the bark of a sycamore.

"Architect? What buildings did you build?"

My new practice was just beginning to distill, so my portfolio hadn't quite risen above the strip shopping center. Currently on the boards, as we said back in the days of the T-square, were drawings of a convenience store and a dry cleaner. Since this wasn't satisfactory bait for new clients, I pulled a rehearsed line out of my pocket.

"I'm forming several design-build partnerships in the area, and I've got two commercial proj – "

"Give me your card," he said. "I've got fifty thousand square feet of dead office space on my balance sheet. I sublet to a bunch of sub-prime mortgage weasels, and they left a God damn mess of it. You can design the build-out as I lease it."

The most lucrative commission I have ever received was given and taken away in the same three minute conversation, throughout which I pried for the name of his company, his card, or a corporate contact, but I was denied even a hair of his DNA. He had *many* business interests and organizations under his guidance. Very complex, he said. He would call me.

As modern human predators often do, and I concede it seemed to be appropriate protocol, he squeezed my hand and came just shy of separating it from my arm. Several of my knuckles popped, and he smiled his flaky smile. It was his way of peeing a circle around himself. I knew I'd never hear from him again.

Wine, drink, and hors d'oeuvres flowed through the crowd on the perched fingertips of waiters in red jackets. They worked mechanically and at times didn't seem human, programed to feed the face and empty the platter, falling just short of stuffing the little canapes and shrimp in our mouths with their fingers. One waiter, anointed with white gloves and a small wand, held a silver tray in the middle of each cluster of people and pointed. On his platter was a long rectangle of purple velvet with little place-names seated around it. A bell rang and dinner was served.

It was obvious a great deal of planning and manipulation went into the seating arrangement. Couples were separated as far as conveniently possible to guard against domestic table talk that might ensue if it happened to be trash night. Lobbyists, Congressman, and other significants were seated concentrically around the ambassador, and journalists were scattered liberally about.

Spouses, 'and guests' were assigned to the ends of the table, so as to bore the least number of significants.

We took our seats and everyone pointed their chins high with anticipation. There was no food on the table – only arrangements of china, crystal, and silver sparkling by dimmed chandeliers and candlelight. On cue, a company of waiters circled the party, topped glasses, filled plates, and took them away as the last bite passed our lips.

Adriane, now bubbly after soaking in a few drinks, was seated at the other end of the table between a congressman on the Commerce Committee and a bearded lobbyist who kept leaning over to put his nose in her ear. Her laughter and my distance from her grew with each encounter with the nose.

Across from me at the end of the table sat a congressman's wife beaming with importance. Her face clung to youth as well as any anyone mired in middle age, but the strings in her neck seemed permanently taut from smiling at too many functions.

"Mr. Miller, you're the architect everyone's talking about this evening. It must be a fascinating profession."

That morning I had been reviewing specs and spatial requirements for dry cleaning equipment.

"Yes," I said. "The art is tremendous."

"I've recently formed a charitable non-profit and I'm planning to locate its headquarters downtown. I'll be needing an architect."

I gave my canned line a rest and simply offered my services. She received me enthusiastically, but said nothing more of her new charity, even after I probed. She spent the next hour asking questions of my life and times. I figured it was part of her interview process, so I didn't mind when she got personal. When I told her Adriane and I were only on our third date, she looked strangely satisfied. She leaned toward me, her sagging dress revealing a perfumed gap below her neck. I had a feeling she wanted to reach across the table and straighten my tie.

"We'll have lunch this week, just you and me," she said. "I'll show you all my desires for the foundation."

"Where would you like to meet?"

"You'll come to my row house in Georgetown. Everything I want to show you is there."

She excused herself to find the ladies room, brushing my shoulder as she passed. When she returned she extended a business card in her open palm the same way the waiters had offered the hors d'oeuvres – as though I might like a taste. This time I thought the deal might go somewhere.

After dinner, cocktails flowed, and the ambassador finished making his rounds. Of all the formal dress and elegance of the evening, this man shone like a lone rose in bouquet of daisies. Perhaps it was his title or knowing he was the temporary guardian of the mansion, but it seemed as though the room had been built around him.

"I want to apologize for my attire," I said. "Adriane called me with little notice."

"Don't worry, my friend, I understand. The cleaners are not always dependable."

I only owned three suits and one no longer fit. I was hoping word of my car hadn't reached the ambassador.

"Please, come with me," he said.

We stepped through the French doors onto the veranda overlooking the gardens. Rain had begun to fall, and the slick stone paths and a few select trees shimmered in the ambient light. A waiter appeared from nowhere and greeted us with a humidor, opening right it under my nose.

"Cohiba?"

This was like a gift to sooth my embarrassment of leaving the tuxedo that I did not own at the cleaners. As an act of charity, the ambassador put two more Cubans in my jacket pocket.

"I understand you are a significant architect."

He was interested in what skyscrapers I had designed. Shutting out thoughts of my latest commission, a tool shed for my neighbor's back yard, I gave him the addresses of several high-rises I worked on years ago as an intern.

The ambassador listened with great attention, nodded and raised his eyebrows on cue, but seemed to look right through me. I had watched him all evening and it appeared to be protocol to engage each guest individually for several minutes. As I was in the middle of trying to dazzle him, he checked his watch and excused himself, apparently having determined his allotted time with me was spent.

Alone on the veranda, I blew wisps of smoke into the moist air and surveyed the gardens as the rising fog slowly obscured my vision. I was imagining the foundation headquarters I would design, though I still knew nothing about it. A velvet-lined contentment wrapped around me, and I felt safe and coddled on the edge of this grand scene. I could get used to this, I dreamed, as the laughter from inside grew louder.

Despite the warmth of Cuban tobacco, the damp evening gave me a sudden chill, and I turned. I hadn't heard the congressman approach from behind. The grey in his temples looked intentionally dyed and gave him an air of false profundity. He stared at me and shook his head, his own half smoked Cohiba smoldering in one hand.

"Do you believe this shit?" he said.

"Hell of a spread." I found myself changing speech patterns to best fit the target audience.

"I go to one of these a month. Ain't nothing I haven't seen and I still don't believe it."

"Don't get used to it," I joked. "It's an election year."

"Pfssh. My daddy held my seat for thirty-four years. By name alone, I'm king." He took a long drag and the embers glowed. "They don't even put anyone else on the ballot anymore."

The man emanated a sense of entitlement, and I stood there trying to imagine such a life.

"Adriane and I go way back." he said. "I still feed her leads over lunch now and then."

"I'm sure her editor appreciates that."

"I don't know about her editor, but I've always left *her* satisfied. You've got to feed the vultures or they'll feed on you." He took out a lighter and stoked his cigar. Between puffs of smoke, he asked, "You fucking her too?"

A cynical air of jealously hung over the two of us as our Cohibas burned.

"Excuse me?" I shot back.

He looked me top to bottom without hiding it. "You're not on The Hill, are you?"

"I'm not sure I want to be on The Hill."

He turned toward the lawn. "No wonder the ambassador was disappointed with the guest list."

Adriane swept through the doors with a drink in hand and rubbed into me in a territorial way. She exchanged glances with the congressman. He shook his head and swaggered down the veranda.

"Yes sir," he said. "This is some shit."

Adriane gave off an aura of victory. She had gone from twitchy to bubbly to saucy, but her hair no longer bounced.

"You wouldn't believe the contacts I'm making tonight. Want to know a secret?" She slid a hand into her dress and pulled out a small writing tablet. "I just got the poop on the new free trade agreement. It's going to be dead in committee." She waved the pad in my face as though playing keep-away. "I scribbled the lead in the bathroom. Did you see the fucking bathroom?"

She stuffed the notebook back in her dress where I hoped to remove it later that evening.

"You have a good rapport with that congressman?" I asked.

"Congressman shit. I don't talk to congressman to find out if a bill is going down." She scowled contemptuously toward the end of the veranda where the king was rounding the corner. "All they're good for are sound bites."

"Are you still doing *lunches* with him?"

Her eyes seemed to ask, "What did he say?" She slid her hand under my jacket and kissed me and bit my lip, marking her turf. I pushed her back, but she centered on my face as though about to reveal a ghastly secret.

"Did you see me talking to the bearded man at dinner? He's a top lobbyist for one of the labor unions."

Adriane was absorbed in the scene as if in the middle of foreplay. I worried that her lobbyist, whose nose spent most of dinner in her ear, had the same credibility as the gentleman with the peeling face who had given me the bogus commission. I had the urge to be alone again with my vanity, but she seized my hand and led me back inside where she continued her mining. Before we passed through the door, she grabbed my cigar and flicked it onto the lawn where it fizzled in the wet grass.

Somewhere between the vodka and the tobacco, the power elite had transformed into caricatures of their public personas – each face a facade as over-designed as the room they were standing in. Couples separated, merged, and buzzed around the vulgar oasis, forming small groups of short lived alliances. Whenever someone joined a flower of people in conversation, the one who had been there the longest parted for another bud. This pollination went on all evening as though it were choreographed by a man in a dark booth.

At a preordained hour, the ambassador gave his goodwill speech and bid us all a safe evening, after which everyone began meandering to the front door. I called for the car, and Adriane and I stood in the foyer with our arms spread as two ushers raised our coats onto our shoulders. The ambassador approached as the valet pulled my car under the portico. He glanced at it before turning to Adriane. Holding her hand, he thanked her for coming and asked her to send his best wishes to his good friend, her editor-in-chief. He shook my hand, as a matter of formality, then turned to the other departing guests.

Before lowering my head into the car, I took a last look at the mansion. The rain left immense drip marks on the limestone facade as if it were melting under the spot lights, reluctantly revealing its inner layers. I slid into my torn vinyl seat. The valet bowed, lowering himself to my level.

"I hope you have had a new and pleasurable evening, sir."

He closed the door.

The moment we passed through the gate, Adriane gushed over the evening. She began dropping the names of all the people she'd met. I thought she might pull out her notepad and start writing her next byline.

"I'm having lunch with that lobbyist next week," she said, as though planning an attack. Then, like someone pricked her with a pin, she took a brief interest in me.

"Tonight should have done wonders for your practice, Lee. You did pick up some contacts, I assume?"

"Yeah, I got one. Maybe a few more."

At the first traffic light, I felt my breast pocket and pulled out the business card the congressman's wife had given me. On fine linen stock it pronounced her charity foundation in elegant script. I flipped it over and on the back was an imprint of her lips in wet pink and a handwritten phone number.

"May I?" Adriane plucked the card out of my hand and held it over the dash to read by the street lights. "This could put you on the map," she said approvingly. I felt her impression of me rise as though I had passed some crucial test. She didn't notice the back of the card.

As I gazed ahead, I saw the congressman's wife across from me again, her leg brushing mine, telling me her desires. We were having lunch, just as her husband and Adriane once did, and I envisioned her building I had not yet designed and began to wonder what was real and what was not real. The traffic light changed and I slowly accelerated. The wipers swept their monotonous squeegees, clearing my vision again and again.

"Who knows," I said, cracking open the window to test the air. "I might be able to get you a few more sound bites from that congressman."

"Really," she laughed. She was still holding the business card, only now face down in her lap. As we passed under each street light, the pink lips on the back of the card flashed like an all-night motel sign. I knew she saw it when her hand covered the card, and the car grew cold. It was like she had suddenly sobered, and we were again driving to the dinner.

"Any other contacts I should know about?" she asked pointedly, tipping the vanity mirror to check the damage.

"That's the only one that sounds like a sure thing," I said demurely. "I'm meeting her this week at her home in Georgetown. You do these high powered lunches all the time, Adriane. What do I have to look forward to?"

Whatever she said in response, I didn't hear. I didn't need to listen anymore. From the corner of my eye I saw her slip the business card into her purse. I knew she would throw it away, relieving me the burden. This would also relieve me the guilt of not calling Adriane again, and perhaps leaving me in regret at the end of the month as I review my books and decide which bills to pay.

Other Fine Gifts

LAST YEAR, despite the growing chill in my home, I was intent on celebrating the season. I took solace in the city and all its festivity, each afternoon stealing an hour after classes to wander downtown in search of the perfect gift. The lampposts trailing down Wisconsin Avenue were garnished with frozen wreaths and red ribbon, and the happy and hurried faces of shoppers blew by like snowflakes in a storm. As I joined a flow of people in front of the bookstore and pushed into the vestibule, a blast of hot air washed over me, but I was warmed on the inside by a familiar face – an old college flame twenty years removed from my life was standing before me with little silver bells dangling from her ears. We stood toe to toe like wooden dolls and blinked at each other.

"Oh my God," she said. "Roger Loughlin?"

But for the crow's feet, Loren possessed the same appeal, both the sexual and the intangible, as she did in college. Her hair bounced lightly on her shoulders and she wore a long cashmere coat that somehow managed to show her figure. She looked like she would drop her bags to hug me, but held on as if she carried some fragile gift. Instead, she grabbed my arm and raised her cheek to mine in a kind of mock kiss that didn't seem to leave either of us satisfied.

"Loren," I said, smiling for the first time in a while. "I heard rumors you were still in town. I never knew where to find you."

"I'm found everywhere, Roger. There's no place I'm not." She still had a spice about her, some tingling energy that always gave me a rise. I stared at her pink cheeks and fumbled for words, but she kept things going. "I heard through the grapevine you got tenure."

"A life sentence," I said.

She looked down and tugged my sleeve. "My God. Is that the same coat you wore in school?"

"I have a few irrational attachments. Coats, old baseball gloves . . . my wife."

"Silly. How's Trish? It is Trish, isn't it?"

I shifted my stance as though casually satisfying an itch. My first thought was that Trish and I were *enduring* each other.

"It's an endearing relationship. Marital bliss, kids, the usual."

"I'm on husband number three and tentatively holding." She gave a little shrug. "I wish husbands were more like Christmas gifts. I can return Christmas gifts."

For a brief second, after catching a familiar glint in her eye, I remembered the night in college I snuck up the dorm stairwell to her room. I was half drunk and out of shape, so I stopped on the way to catch my breath, dodging into one of the dorm's kitchens. I raided the refrigerator for beer, but it was dry, so I opened the freezer and found a big chunk of meat. I grabbed it and ran the rest of the stairs to her door, where I made up a secret knock. She pulled me in, locked the door behind us, and ground into me. It didn't take her long to find the cold lump under my coat. "What's that?" she asked between kisses. "A gift," I said. "I think it's a pot roast."

Now Loren stood before me like a freshly trimmed tree. Her smell triggered old memories, but what did I really know of her anymore? All our intimate moments were buried under three husbands and countless hairstyles. Though I wondered what it would be like to be with her again, it saddened me to realize that all of my old impressions were open for question. She was the same, but different, wearing the immeasurable of what she had become.

She kept staring at my coat. "There are a lot of things I would return if I could," she said quietly. She touched on bits of her life, graced with an occasional reference to our college days that would cause us both to smile and blush. We exchanged phone numbers and agreed to do lunch one day, but when we parted she cupped my hand and said goodbye as though there would soon be another twenty years between us.

She left me to peruse the book shelves, and my eyes passed aimlessly over the titles with no more interest than folding laundry. I was stuck on the idea of returning things, of going back and starting over. Loren and I had always been on and off, and I think that in my lair of insecurities, I considered her a backup in case I didn't find anyone. That illusion was shattered after graduation when she married her first husband and dropped away into life. Grad school proved to be a cold replacement. I spent my dissertation wavering between bad dates and solitude, until loneliness, that great motivator of simple men, compelled me to marry.

Needing to clear my head, I spent the next hour wandering the tree-lined streets of Georgetown, sneaking glances through windows of majestic brick row houses, so I might live vicariously in someone else's life. I contemplated my failures and trails not taken. I eventually found myself in front of Georgetown University, the place I always considered the origin of my adult wanderings. From where I stood, I could see my office window, as well as Loren's old dormitory, the path between full of unexpected turns.

Noticing the hour, I left for home down P Street. Abandoned trolley rails sliced the street into alternating bands of cobblestone and steel, and I followed the old line east and watched the rails eventually break and fade under Wisconsin Avenue. There was never an evening I crossed that intersection when I didn't wonder where the lines had gone in their prime. The trolleys were scrapped in the '60s, part of the city's blood-line severed.

∞

A narrow brick alley runs beside my house and I always felt it was more satisfying to bypass the front foyer and follow the enveloping alley to the back door off the kitchen. That evening, after pausing a moment to peer through the window, I took a deep breath and went inside. I felt the house's age as I shut the door. Warmth seemed to seep away through every crack and joint, and I stood where all the cool drafts converged.

I hung up my coat and cap, and rustled my remaining hair back to life. The coat was a down-filled trash bag twenty years out of style, but it was a skin in which I always felt comfortable. Trish let me wear it in public only when I was alone.

"You didn't pick them up?" Trish whisked into the kitchen in her business suit and stocking feet. She took control of the room, opening and closing cabinet doors as if she were the only one authorized to do so.

"They're staying after school," I said. "They have a ride. We discussed this last night." She took a can of string beans from the cabinet and examined the label.

"You didn't shop, did you?"

"I couldn't find anything that struck me."

"That's the problem. You're always looking for things that strike *you*."

"Let's not start this again." I felt the muscles in my face begin to tighten.

"You should look for things that are striking to *them*. Not bows and coconuts. Fine gifts they were."

"They seemed to like them okay," I replied weakly.

"I've taken care of the shopping."

I sighed, shook my head. Things had been this way for the past year, and I was beginning to wear down. "So what are we getting them?"

"TVs for their rooms. And they're each getting the newest video games."

"Video games? Christ."

"And I have two each of those scooters hidden in the trunk of the car, so don't let them go snooping around."

The city was full of pot holes, busted sidewalks, and cobble stones. Where did she expect them to scoot? I watched her put a block of frozen ground beef in the microwave and push "defrost."

"You should learn to spend more quality time with them," she said.

I wanted to storm the hell out of there, go back to the bookstore, anywhere, maybe call Loren, but I just retreated to the den and sank into a soft chair. For Trish it was all about the latest fad, what was *in*. I had tried to explain to her that the gift is in their perception, in what they do with things, what they *make* of them.

The prior Christmas I marveled as my son Ross contemplated his coconut. He started by puzzling over the mysterious slushing inside. Then he spent the winter in the basement hurling it in a make-shift bowling alley at any of his toys that would stand. By spring it was dried out and cracked, the husk ready for peeling. I watched him tear the outer casing away and squeal. He held the hairy ball in the air like he'd found a secret treasure. After pulling the hairs off the shell and placing them in a pin box for safekeeping, it was time for the inner fluid to be liberated. He tried the side of a tree, rocks, both round and sharp, and finally a fling out the upper bedroom window. I remember the milk splashing on Trish's car.

My daughter Jamie's gift was just as much fun to watch in all its incarnations. I gave her a spool of red ribbon, the most beautiful glowing hue you could imagine. I found it at an industrial surplus – a bolt of 1,000 linear feet, and I gave her reign over the house. With no more than her hands and a pair of scissors, she bowed and draped everything in sight for six months. I took the closet doors down in her bedroom so she could replace them with dangling red streamers. She wrapped all the old radiators in the house in neo-*De Stijl* compositions, and with quick wisps of her scissors, she made curly shavings for punk doll hair and garnishes for her cap. Once, when I was sick, I woke to find bows on my toes.

The house shook as Jamie and Ross burst through the back door in a cold huff, mittens and boots flying. Through the door I saw Trish give each a hug, which did remind me where her heart was, though I couldn't recall the last time I received such affection.

"You two get washed and ready for dinner," I heard her say.

The two of them tumbled into the den. Jamie, still wearing her cap with a curl of red, gave me a peck on the cheek and plopped into a chair with her book-bag. Ross, his nose running and face flush from the cold, made for the television.

"Homework first." I said. After a quick and exaggerated sulk, he turned to me.

"Daddy, why do you have a bald spot?"

"It's a sign of good luck. Pat it and your wish comes true."

"It does not."

"Sure it does."

"Jamie said you have a bald spot because you're smart."

"She's not lying. Just stretching the imagination." Jamie looked up from her homework with a sly smile and twirled her hair with a pencil.

Ross came to my side and put his little hand to my crown. "Pat, pat, pat," he said.

"Having any luck?" I glanced at his red face from the corner of my eye.

"I don't know."

"You've got to make a wish, stupid," Jamie said.

"Jamie." I gave her an eye.

"Sorry. What's for dinner?"

"Your mother is making meatloaf."

Ross pulled his hand away. "Nope, it doesn't work." He grabbed his book bag and ran upstairs.

∞

That Christmas, the last in my own home, Trish gave me a book, "101 Things To Do With Your Children," and a six-pack of tube socks. Three weeks later she threw me out, another blood-line severed.

I left through the front foyer like an unwanted guest, the door slamming harder than I intended, which shamed me for probably scaring the kids. I walked the root-cracked sidewalk in the January freeze, hailed a cab on M Street, and cried a hemorrhaging fit all the way to a motel in Arlington. I carried two suitcases, both of which Trish had packed, and two books: an old family bible and a book on Socrates. I grabbed them on the way out in a sad attempt to take a piece of that life with me. I don't know why I choose those two, but I remember wanting to keep things simple. I told myself that one was about a carpenter, the other about a man who spent his life asking questions.

∞

Trish announced her engagement right after the following Thanksgiving. After the gut illness of the first few days passed, it was no big deal. A relief, really. But on that first lamenting day I tortured over the past, going on long walks with my old coat enveloping me like a security blanket. All these years I was just passing time, losing my hair, under the illusion of marital tenure.

I went back to the bookstore on Wisconsin Avenue and stared blankly into the stacks, just as I did after my encounter with Loren. And it occurred to me that Loren and I had broken up for the last time the week after I snuck up the stairs to her dorm room. One stupid question flashed into my head: How could I not have asked her about the pot roast? Did she eat it? Was it tender? Did she make a nice brown gravy with it? Did she share it with another guy? What in God's name did she do with the pot roast? At that moment, I think I would have exchanged all my gifts for another shot.

That evening I sat on a plastic kitchen chair in my one-bedroom apartment, eating some sort of processed microwave meat food. I had carried her number in my wallet since the day I saw her, and now it was laying on the table by the phone. I could pick it up and call her any time. No reason I shouldn't.

I was wearing the leather bracelet Jamie had given me for Christmas the year before, and I turned it around my wrist. She made it in art class, and it had my name embossed on one side and the words "Know Yourself" on the other. Across the kitchen table sat Ross's present, a birdhouse he made from scrap wood. The roof was slightly skewed and the perch was the stub of a #2 pencil with a drip of paint sagging from the tip. He put the last of the coconut hairs inside 'to give the birds a head start,' he had said, but the house sat unoccupied, sheltering nothing. I stirred my food and looked at my bracelet and birdhouse, and it occurred to me these were the most beautiful things in my world.

∞

On Constitution Avenue, at the foot of the National Archives, lies a ring of ice with skaters circling, some hand-in-hand, others meandering as though searching for nothing at all. The Hirshhorn Museum, like a conscience, watches from across the Mall with a stern eye. Ross sat on the bench with his skate between my legs as I wrestled with his laces. Jamie was tying her own behind me.

"Tie them tight, Jamie. Real tight," I said over my shoulder.

"But they hurt when they're too tight."

"Well, not that tight. Trust me. You want to get it just right."

"If I don't get it right, I can always go back and do it over."

I paused.

"Just do the best you can, sweetie."

The Zamboni hummed across the ice and wiped away the old tracks, leaving shining wet ribbons in its wake. Jamie and Ross were poised at the gate, ready. A whistle blew and play resumed, silver blades kicking.

"Look, Dad! I'll make a figure eight," Jamie called.

"Bet'cha can't." Ross hot-dogged by her.

"Can too!" Jamie whipped her head toward me in revelation. "Daddy, pat your bald spot for me! Pat your head good luck!"

With one skate on, the other limp on the rubber mat, I dropped my laces and patted my shining crown, mustering all the forces of good luck at my disposal.

Jamie bent and wobbled on one leg, arms spread soaring, a slow motion sail. Ross, ever chiding, glided around her without even trying. Their gifts were known and I was their origin, and there was nothing behind them nor safety net below. I kept patting my head, watching them spin away from my cold feet, carelessly slicing their trails in the virgin ice. Don't stop, I whispered to no one. Please don't ever stop. Let me see where you go.

The Waters of Casablanca

FREYDOON CAME HERE FROM IRAN just before the revolution. Along the way he tended bar from Karachi to Cairo to Frankfurt, and somewhere in the process he converted from Islam to the dollar. Now he ran the best bar in Georgetown. Always stoic and gracious, he was the kind of man who would gladly carry you in conversation if you looked like you needed carrying. He could also sense when you wanted to be left the hell alone. Freydoon was a man I could trust.

As I walked in the door, I caught his familiar dark eyes and he poured me a draft. I was meeting my friend Mike, as I did every Friday afternoon, to discuss the latest in politics and homeland security over a quiet drink before the crush of happy hour. I was late but so was Mike, which was out of character. I grabbed one of the last stools and scanned the bar. Freydoon's narrow storefront ran deep to the alley with a line of round tables paralleling the bar to the kitchen.

Everything was oak, but the bar-top was sealed with so many layers of polyurethane it no longer resembled wood, let alone oak. Freydoon set the beer in front of me as a line of suds trailed down the glass and disappeared into a square napkin. The first mouthful was sharp in my throat, but after a few sips, it tasted like water.

"How about the *tortellini en brodo*?" I said.

"Good." Freydoon went to the kitchen window and gave the order to his chef.

The front door blew open, and Mike walked in with his tie and collar already loose. He looked like he had just woken from a nap on the floor. His ID badge bounced from side to side on his chest as he tossed his keys on the bar.

"Plan on staying?" I asked.

"Don't let me drive home."

He passed behind me and disappeared into the men's room. I exchanged a concerned glance with Freydoon as he dropped a napkin next to the keys and went to the tap. I was on my second round before Mike came back and twisted onto his stool. He pulled a cigarette box from his coat and nodded thanks to Freydoon, who kept watch behind the bar like a wooden Indian.

"I assume you didn't come from the Bureau?" I said.

He shook his head no and fumbled with his lighter. "I've been out since lunch. Had a few at the Old Ebbitt."

"A half day? We're at war, Mike. What would J. Edgar have said?"

"J. Edgar wouldn't be dicking around like these PC assholes." With that, he swallowed half his beer and placed the glass carefully on the napkin.

"I thought you were cutting back," I said. I picked up his keys and slipped them in my pocket.

"You don't know what I know."

"Come on. How bad could it be? It's Friday night."

"Barbarians at the gates, Lou." Mike stared at his face in the mirror behind the bar and held on to his glass and cigarette like he was holding on to the ledge of a tall building. "They put me on administrative leave this morning."

"What the hell for?"

"Something about my investigative techniques falling short of the Bill of Rights."

"Shit. What happens now?"

"Closed door meetings, a hearing or two, a reprimand. They'll try to make it bad enough for me to quit."

"Don't sweat it. Just go through the motions."

"They've tied my hands." Mike rubbed his forehead with the base of his palm, his cigarette coming dangerously close to igniting his hair. "If we don't come down hard on these Wahhabis, in a hundred years there won't be a Bill of Rights to defend."

Freydoon, apparently sensing a man in need, placed himself between Mike and his reflection. He planted his two hands flat on the bar. "I went to Rome last year, Michael. And I went to Ostia. Do you know Ostia?" Mike shook his head that he did not. "No matter. Ostia is just another abandoned Roman town. Ruins is all. As I was touring this town, I came across what was at one time a local bar. It had a long stone counter, an open space for tables and chairs, and a kitchen, just like this place." He waved a hand around in the air as though it might help Mike understand. "So right there I realized, two thousand years ago after a long day at work, people went to this bar to eat and drink and smoke and bullshit and hit on women, just like you two are doing right now."

"We haven't hit on any women yet," Mike said as smoke rose from his lips.

"The night is young. The point is the cycle of daily life is never broken. Let this flavor of Muslim and their jihad do what they will. They will fight you, and you will fight them, and no matter who wins, two thousand years from now our descendants will go to bars after work and eat and drink and smoke and bullshit and hit on women."

"I'll report your findings to the Director."

Down from Mike at the end of the bar sat a gentleman in his sixties wearing a heavy wool sport coat too hot for the season. Sweat beaded on his forehead, and he wore a wiry beard that looked like it had been pulled out of his back. His lips were parted as if paused, ready to interject.

"Go ahead and worry," Freydoon said, trailing back to the kitchen window. "That is your job."

"It is my job to worry," Mike said, reassuring himself.

"And it is my job to know why," the older man said as he folded his hairy hands into an attentive ball in front of his martini. He spoke in a clean Euro-something accent, but there was something unclean about him, as if he showered only once a week. Mike regarded him with suspicion.

"And you are?"

"Oliver Ryckaert." He offered his hand over a vacant stool, and Mike hesitated before shaking it. "I'm a journalist."

"Where from?" I asked.

"I am from Belgium," he said. Then he took a closer interest in Mike. "I assume you are in security?"

"Your security," Mike said.

"Then we are on the same side. I know since I overheard the talk of women and drink."

Mike smiled for the first time and signaled Freydoon for another round. "So what are you reporting to your Belgian friends back home?"

"The shining star that is America lives. Or the baffling arrogance that is America. It depends on who I'm writing for."

"You can tell them we're doing just fine."

"Then why so worried?"

It was Mike's job to worry, but not to talk. It was stupid for him to engage this guy, especially under suspension, but the drinks from his long lunch were already in him and he started talking more than he should have. Oliver slid over a stool, and the two became engrossed with each other. Then I remembered an earlier conversation when Mike pontificated about the benefit of a man in his position having discreet media contacts. To me the relationship sounded more like a pair of apes combing each other for fleas. With this in mind, I kept to myself. Freydoon brought me my bowl of *tortellini en brodo*, and I ate quietly and listened. Over the next hour, the temperature and music volume rose, and the happy hour crowd filled the bar and bumped into our backs. Freydoon passed drinks to them over our shoulders.

"You have no idea how many cells we've identified," Mike said over the crowd to Oliver. "They're smart, and they're patient. We can watch them, but we can't do a damn thing until they do something first."

"Well, then you have them."

"Some."

"But when they strike, you will have them and their associates. We are talking about a finite number."

"But how many will they kill? How many people will we lose in the process?"

"If man wants to kill and has half a mind, man will kill, but most will expose themselves."

"We work from the underappreciated view that no one gets killed."

"You are trying to deny future historians of good material. But never mind that," Oliver said, waving his hand. "Man's nature will not let the historians down." The crowd was getting louder, and people began pushing into one another to get to the bar. Oliver crouched under someone's extended arm and said, "Would you gentleman like a taste of a parallel civilization?"

Mike looked at me and I shrugged.

"Come. It is a mere block from here. My treat, as you say." Oliver unfolded several bills from a silver money clip and laid them on the bar. We nodded to Freydoon, and he punched in our tab. He brought the receipt and leaned toward me.

"Shall I call a cab for Michael?"

"No," I said. "I'll take care of him."

Freydoon grabbed two more glasses to be filled. "Be at peace, Michael," he called out to him. As Mike passed through the door, he glanced back at Freydoon as though the idea of peace belonged to a different epic.

Outside on M Street the traffic revved by and the air felt as thick as the Potomac. The street lamps had just lighted in the dusk and cast their dank glow through the humidity. The three of us gathered together on the narrow sidewalk in front of Freydoon's. Oliver took a deep breath like it was a fresh spring day, then turned and led us for a block before stepping into a sunken doorway. The storefront was blacked out, and over the front door a sign with small hand-painted letters read, *The Waters of Casablanca*. Mike eyed me that this was not good. I told him to come on, and he tucked his ID badge in his front pocket.

Oliver was warmly greeted by a white robed maître d' whose checkered scarf spiraled from his head and rested on one shoulder. They spoke quietly to each other and nodded at me and Mike as we stared blankly around the room. The tables were spaced far apart and full of dark-skinned families with children sitting quiet and dignified. The maître d' stepped toward us, presented his right palm, and asked us to please follow. We wove through the tables to the back of the restaurant where a waiter stood watch at a door. He made eye contact with the maître d', then bowed and opened the door to a stair that double-backed toward the front of the restaurant. The stair descended into darkness and out of the darkness came the percussive wailing of drums and an accompanying flute. Oliver let out a sigh and descended first. We felt along the walls with our hands, and at the bottom landing we pushed aside several heavy curtains and entered a large room that could have been the inside of a Bedouin's tent. The ceiling and walls were draped with blankets and sheets, and it was warm – not warm like outside, but warm like being wrapped in swaddling bands in your mother's lap. The tables were low, and bearded men with clothed heads sat on silk cushions and ate from bowls with their fingers. Two dancers circled the room to the din of the music, one in lavender, the other in glittering turquoise, and presented themselves to one table at a time.

A new maître d' showed me to a half vacant table where Oliver was lowering himself to the floor. He sank into the pillows and seemed comfortable, though he had not lost his ungainly appearance. Mike and I sat, and had a time of it. Mike is not what I would call 'flexible'. He could barely cross his legs and ended up extending them adjacent to the table with his black polished wingtips pointing awkwardly into the air and the soles of his feet offending everyone at the next table. I shifted and shuffled the cushions like I was having a sleepless night. Two Arab men sitting at our table gave us tight-lipped smiles and gestured to share their bowls of food.

Mike leaned over to my ear. "I shouldn't be here."

"It's just another bar," I said, though as I stared around the room, I wasn't sure I was being entirely honest. "Don't worry about it."

Oliver was elated. He looked at us with his mouth grinning wide and turned back to the belly dancers twisting around the room. Mike leaned in closer.

"One of the cells I was watching was out of Morocco," he said, and I was afraid he said it too loud. Oliver listed toward us.

"Can you gentleman tell me the difference between here and Freydoon's?" It was a rhetorical question as he turned away, plucked a kabob from a bowl, and popped it into his mouth.

Mike examined the bowls of food on the table. "What the hell is this stuff?"

"Will you relax?" I said. "I'd rather not be thrown out." I was too buzzed to deal with being thrown out, and I had finally found a comfortable pose in the pillows. Oliver had already ordered, and a boy waiter appeared. He had strong blue eyes and an eagerness to please, and carried himself with a youthful grace that is often lost to suspicion as one ages. He carried a tray with three drinks to the table and sat one in front of each of us. I raised the small cup to my nose and inhaled its mint vapor, then sipped it and let the spice warm my throat. My eyes wandered and caught others staring as if our presence had altered some delicate equilibrium. The boy seemed to sense our awkwardness; shepherding us like we were lost sheep, he was never far away.

As soon as I finished my tea, he was there with his tray to replace my cup. He bent down toward Mike like he was presenting an offering. Mike wouldn't even look at him. After scanning the room as if memorizing faces, his eyes came back to the incense smoldering from an urn in the center of the table. He waved the boy off. "I'm not ready," he said.

The music droned on like a primal scream, and the dancers gave the illusion that the whole tent was moving to some outside sandstorm. Mike kept glancing back toward one corner of the room. He finally motioned to me and put a hand to the side of his mouth.

"I need to get out of here, Lou. Give me my keys."

"You're too drunk."

He slowly enunciated his words. "Give - me - my - keys."

"You recognize someone?" I dug into my pocket, and when I felt only lint, I checked the others and found coins and a breath mint. Before Mike could respond, I looked him in the eyes and braced for his reaction. "I think they're gone."

"Shit," he said over the music. He started feeling his own pockets. "I swear that God damn maître d' put his hands on us when we walked by."

Though most of the room was now staring at us, Mike singled out a man in a black turban sitting right behind me. His beard was perfectly trimmed, and his lips were bent somewhere between mischievousness and repose.

"What the hell are you looking at?" Mike said.

The man raised his left arm as if about to perform magic, then opened his fist one finger at a time. "I believe these are yours," he said. "They were shining between the cushions. It is apparent they slipped out of your friend's pocket."

Mike grabbed the keys and buried them in his own pocket, as though he was not sure if he was dealing with a petty thief or a good Samaritan. He picked up his cup of tea and sniffed, then set it down.

"Relax, Mike," I whispered. "Who did you see?"

After one last flash around the room, he dropped a five dollar bill on the table. "Don't follow me," he said. He stood and, being careful not to step on anyone, ambled toward the stair and had a time finding his way through the curtains.

Oliver didn't even notice. A dancer was spinning in front of him, throwing her scarves and pinching her dark eyes through her veil. He sat before her rocking and clapping, bouncing up and down on his pillow in a celebrant wonder like he had just found God. He raised his glass and shouted over the music, "This is all of mans' wants!"

Left in the residue of Mike's distrust, I stared around the room and sensed that half the men were looking at the dancers and the other half were looking at me. My mind filled with images of hidden daggers under cloaks, and poison, and plots not yet executed. I glanced over my shoulder at the man who returned Mike's keys and found his eyes black and distant. Then in a chill, like a drop of cold water down my spine, I thought to myself I could never know him. I wondered how I could ever know any of them.

Mike had asked me not to follow, but at this point, as an embarrassed guest nesting in the warm den of suspicion, I could not see following anyone. The mint tea had settled me, and I sank into the softness of the place and felt watched and didn't care. Like Oliver, my eyes focused on the dancers as they surrounded our table and wound to the static percussion of the drums. They cast their scarves to capture men and moved like snakes and showed some parts and hid others, always moving and hiding, exposing only enough to keep us in wait. It was the same dance for two thousand years, and they would dance for two thousand more.

I raised my tea, but tasted only salt from my lips. As I lowered the empty cup, the boy waiter appeared again in peaceful repose. He stood by me like a friend, ready and gracious, a reflection of Freydoon in younger days. Under the churning storm clouds of lavender and turquoise I reached out to him, to his blue eyes and his innocence. His smile widened in understanding, and he offered me another drink from his tray as if saying "trust me."

The Transfiguration of Mauricio

MAURICE SANTILLI CONVERTED to Catholicism for the architecture. *Converted* is perhaps the wrong word, for the boy had nothing to convert from. His father, Henry, an American foreign service officer recently based in Rome, would have nothing to do with any God or His messengers and was faithful only in exposing the scriptures as fable and folly. Maurice was not even able to gain a foothold as an atheist as one must at least ponder the existence of God before actually rejecting Him. God was off the table in the Santilli flat – He and Maurice were not even introduced.

Though he didn't know it at the time, Maurice's conversion began on the evening of his twelfth birthday, coming to him in the gift of pastels and a pad of *Fabriano* paper. His mother, Adele, who had taken to calling him Mauricio as soon as they landed in Rome, watched eagerly from the edge of the sofa as he opened the package. His father seemed only to endure the ritual as he balanced a tumbler of vodka on the arm of his leather club chair. Within the wrapping was a sleek wooden box that felt as if it might hold something fragile or of delicate balance. The box alone was a kind of art. Maurice lifted its slender lid to find fifty *Sennelier* oil pastels, the tip of each angled like a Bishop's miter. He plucked a red stave from its slot and ran a line down the first page of *Fabriano*, then varied the weight and angle, experimenting with the color and paper and the new feeling in his hand.

"Rome is the greatest city in the world to draw," his mother said.

Later that night the boy wetted his sheets with sweat. His angular room had only one window and no cross ventilation, so the space was full of shadow and dead air. The distant chatter and clinking of dishes from the café below only reminded him he was alone again in another strange city. Unable to sleep, he crept bare-chested to the window where a street lamp lit his pale skin. The few stars that hadn't been washed out from the lights of the *Campus Martius* shone dimly to the south where the last tourists were shuffling away from *Piazza Navona*. To the north, set ablaze on an intimate piazza, was the spot-lit church that had caught Maurice's attention the day his family moved into the flat.

He straddled the window and found some relief from the cool stone sill along his thigh and calf. Stone was everywhere here. Very different from his father's last assignment in Washington, DC, where their suburban house was sheathed in vinyl siding, and brick was used only as cake dressing. The glowing stone church made him think of a stage set or a kind of carnival celebration. It was less building than sculpture. He imagined the interior was cool, and he longed to be enveloped in stone. He recalled his father's comment that the insides of churches were empty shells, devoid of substance, but Maurice imagined that *Santa Maria della Pace* might have been carved from a single block of stone. Just as the pyramids were solid, so he reasoned something this small could be as well.

The boy opened his new pad of *Fabriano* and began sketching the order and assemblage of the church. He blocked out the facade, taking care of the odd curves and concave wings, sensing the depth of the panels and the circular portico. He repositioned his leg as he worked, rolling his pale calf to a fresh cool spot on the stone window sill. When he reached for the new box of pastels, the spotlights clicked off and left the street in sudden darkness. Only a single street lamp warmed the portico like a child's nightlight. The domed silhouette was left pressing against the sky.

∞

"Why are you bothering with this?" Henry Santilli asked the next morning as he held out the boy's sketch pad.

"Let him draw what he wants," his mother said, nursing an *espresso* over the Herald Tribune. "What else is he supposed to draw from his window?"

"He should have been in bed."

"I couldn't sleep," Maurice said. "It's too hot in there." He hoped placing blame on their new home might deflect his father's criticism, and also apply a little guilt for moving the family again.

Henry tossed the outlined image of the church on the table. "We'll get you a fan," he said, scanning the headlines. "If you can't sleep you should be reading. Have you started the Nietzsche I gave you?"

"No, sir," he said.

"He doesn't need to be reading that at his age," his mother said.

"How about the Machiavelli? Read *The Prince* and I'll take you to Florence and introduce you to the Medicis."

The boy grabbed a croissant and his sketch pad and tried to make a quick exit, but his father called out to him, "Wait. Take this with you." He grabbed a book from the bureau. It was an old copy of Nietzsche's *The Birth of Tragedy*, and he tossed it to him. "I don't want to see you without a book in your hand."

"Yes, sir."

"Be home by five o'clock."

"Yes, sir."

Maurice trotted down the dim stairwell and emerged on *via della Pace*, where the street ended with the flourish of the little parish church. The top bays of the facade were lit by the morning sun, but the iron gated portico, shackled as usual, was still in shadow. He studied it for a moment, considering the lines from a lower perspective, before noticing the old man in grey work clothes sweeping ancient dust from the portico. He worked the broom as if each stroke were tied to some fragile destiny. The man's white hair was upswept and his creviced face made lines crawling skyward. The caretaker's eyes met Maurice's, and the two stared at each other for an awkward moment. Unnerved at being watched by such a face, the boy broke south through the stone laden streets.

∞

For the week since they had moved into their oppressive flat, Maurice had been free to walk the streets and had etched a mental map of the *Campus Martius*. The old city was an emerging mystery to him. He had never seen streets so confined or neighborhoods so intimate. And he noticed that churches, which are legion in Rome, were a kind of anchor, always an event of place or a snag in the urban fabric. On this morning he paused at every church, comparing each with the one on *via della Pace*, which he now considered *his* church. He realized that with familiarity comes a kind of ownership. *Santa Maria della Pace* would forever be his church – all this without him ever setting foot inside.

He emerged from the narrow canyon streets onto *Corso Vittorio Emanuele*, a sudden plague of traffic and diesel fumes. After walking to the *Tevere* and back, he flopped on the sidewalk under the shelter of a café awning where across the street an imposing Baroque church was staring down on him. He studied its facade. Its sheer size made him feel small and lonely and reminded him that he had no friends in Rome. He felt a growing resentment toward his father at being immersed in yet another strange new city.

All the while, people were milling in and out of *Sant'Andrea della Valle*. A few were in suits and dresses, but most wore casual clothes with cameras hanging around their necks. He suspected that there were papers to present and ledgers to sign before one could go inside to do what was called worship. Maurice didn't yet have his student ID card, and his passport was in a safe at the embassy. The only toll collector in sight was the bosomy well-fed gypsy sitting in the doorway, who seemed to pray only to her own secret God.

Maurice imagined his father's wrath as he approached the portal. He stepped over the threshold, past the gypsy's outstretched hands into a coolness he longed for and a space he had never expected. His eyes grew accustomed to the light and were drawn into the enormity of the nave and the marble clad walls, piers, and arches that suspended it all above him. He was standing there in awe, holding a sweating can of Coke when a short, pimple-headed man rushed to his side and began jabbering in Italian and waving his hands. Like a strict headmaster, he tugged once on Maurice's shorts and pointed to a sign by the door that had instructions in four languages and poorly rendered symbols for the illiterate. No shorts, no halter tops, and no food or drink. The man guided him to the door and gave a gentle but conclusive shove into the August heat.

The next day Maurice returned, this time in long pants. He was worried the man might throw him out again or question what he wanted. He didn't know what he wanted, but he knew he hadn't seen enough. The space had christened his interest and made him devout in the desire to walk the nave and stand under the round light he had only sensed from just inside the doors. This time, after passing the same bosomy gypsy, Maurice stood by the first chapel and waited for his ejection that did not come. The light and colors of the space were nothing he had imagined and the interior orders were both as elaborate and as disciplined as its facade. He was amazed at the scale and soon urged himself down the nave with his eyes fastened high as he came under the circle of light. He hadn't seen the dome from the street, and its surprise left him turning in circles under it, feeling as though he might be swept up into the vortex of high drama painted on its underside. When his neck grew stiff, he explored the chapels and their paintings, sculptures and bas reliefs, each a gallery on par with any museum he had ever seen. In his wonder and surprise, it occurred to him that his father was a liar.

∞

He had heard of Jesus only in passing, and had even heard rumors of a ghost, which sounded the least believable of all. Overheard phrases from proverbs and psalms left obvious moral clues to a life well lived, but their origin was unknown to him. Characters from the Bible, from Jacob to Job to Jesus, were inaccessible, less than the flesh and bone of the living or the stone and mortar built in God's name. The idea of heaven and hell held less sway over his soul than what pressed on the three dimensions of his surroundings. Walls, floors and ceilings were what framed his existence and the life he was living, and it was with these surfaces he began his study of God.

He attended his first Mass by accident. In a small church near *Santa Maria Maggiori*, far flung from his parent's flat, he sat quietly in the small congregation and was mesmerized by the language being sung and how it affected the air. The bench was hard and straight-backed, the stone ever-present, but the chant and treble of the celebrants' voices softened his pose. Now sound was a part of the architecture. He immediately began sketching the space. The man's voice from the altar came from all directions, bouncing off every surface. Maurice surveyed the space, trying to discover this play on acoustics, admiring the long dead master builders as they played their subtle tricks.

What alarmed him about Mass was the surprise advance on the altar. Row by row the parishioners approached the man in robes as if lined up for sacrifice. Assistants stood on either side of the celebrant, one holding a plate and the other a silver cup. Maurice felt flush as the line moved forward. This was where they punched his ticket, he thought. As he stood in line he wanted to run. When the woman in front of him stepped aside, he came face to face with the priest who was enormous in his layered robes. A small pale cracker was extended toward his face and Maurice was uncertain what to do. The priest placed it in his hand, then laid his palms on the boy's head. Warm and damp, Maurice felt their imprint on his forehead long after he got back to his seat. The experience wasn't all together unpleasant, but he still vowed to leave the next time before this odd procession began.

Outside after Mass, the music was still with him. He meandered through the streets and spotted bits of pagan empire ruin digested within the city of the church. On realizing the beauty of the centuries stacked on top of one another, he felt there was something more that held it all together. So many had been driven to create. When building in stone wasn't enough, there was painting and fresco and intricate mosaics. Something there inspired people to build – they would not stop laying stones for God.

∞

When he got back to his family's street, he noticed a door to the left of *Santa Maria della Pace* was open. His father wasn't due home for another hour, so he hurried over and stepped inside. He followed the light through two unadorned rooms and passed into a cloister populated with college students. They were sitting on the steps around the perimeter of the arcade, working intently on their sketch pads. Maurice held his drawings behind his back as he regarded the older students' work, comparing their more mature studies to his own. He was startled when a door creaked open behind him. The old man who had been sweeping the portico stepped from a dark room looking like he'd just woken from *siesta*. Maurice stepped aside as the old man mumbled, "*Attento, ragazzo*." He locked the door and trudged down the arcade. "*Tutti i Bramante piccoli*," he said.

Maurice followed at a distance and watched him pass through a tall door into the sanctuary. The door was left cracked open, and the boy knew he needed to go through it. The hinges creaked loudly as he pushed inside.

"*E'chiusa!*" came the caretaker's voice trilling through the nave. He came into view and made a shooing gesture with his hands, as if clearing the space of pigeons. "*Chiuso!*"

The boy just stood there, knowing he was on the threshold of something.

"Closed," the old man tried in English.

"But you're always closed," Maurice countered.

The caretaker paused, as if to consider. "Si. I suppose we are." The old man studied Maurice as he craned his neck toward the dome. "*Va bene,*" the old man relented. "Come in, come in." He stepped across the altar and raised a finger. "I have been watching you. You are the new boy who sits in the window at night."

The caretaker was missing numerous back teeth, making the sides of his cheeks retreat as he spoke. Up close he resembled a sculpture Maurice had seen in the *Capitoline Museum* of a Roman slave in distress, open mouth, hot breath escaping, a long life spent in the service of others.

Maurice stepped under the dome and stared into it as if into a giant kaleidoscope. It was much smaller than *Sant'Andrea*, but no less monumental. The nave before him was short but intimate, with bas relief marble panels mounted by warm frescos. He imagined the congregation and songs and murmuring voices.

"You like the dome," the old man said. "You build your own one day."

"How old is it?"

"Many many years. Many builders. They were scavengers of architecture. You see the chapel?" He gesticulated his arm up and down at the first side altar as he lumbered through the nave. "The Temple of Jupiter

Capitolinus. Rome built for their Gods, we borrow for ours."

"This is where the temples went?"

"Many many temples are in the churches. Their stone is our stone." The caretaker was getting excited as his audience of one followed in his steps. "You know Raphael, *si*?" He escorted the boy to the last altar near the entrance and pointed to the fresco above it. "Forget Michelangelo. You want to draw like Raphael. Nowhere in Rome will you find such a fresco. See the four beautiful women? The Sibyls? They are prophesying with the angels. The one on the left foresaw the coming of Christ. Now they are all angels."

Maurice studied the fresco and knew he would use his pastels here. He sat opposite the chapel and opened his sketch book, but didn't apply the first line before the old man called his attention back to the high altar.

"Madonna and Child," he said, crossing himself toward the old painting framed within the altar. "Throw a stone and she will bleed."

"That's impossible," the boy said.

"It was a miracle. We build in tribute to our miracles. Make homes for them so there might be more in the future."

"Who threw the stone?"

"A nonbeliever. But he believed after he saw her blood."

Maurice studied the faded oil of the woman, but found no scar or any sign of miracle that had inspired the church. "It's just a painting," he said.

"It is not a painting. It is faith. Has your father not taught you faith?"

"He doesn't believe in churches."

The old caretaker reflected for a moment. "So he does not pray?"

"No."

"Does he believe in hope?"

The boy shrugged.

"Hope is a kind of prayer. There is nothing wrong with hope." The caretaker seemed to ponder the thought. "I must go now," he said. "You want to come here to make your art, I leave the side door unlocked until dinner. You may come any day, but tell no one."

∞

Henry Santilli sat in his leather chair and thumbed through a case of files from his old assignments. He pulled out the most worn envelope, which covered his term in Liberia, one of the hardship tours the State Department sends its recruits to learn the way not to run a civilization. He spent two years in Monrovia navigating the war lords and death squads, mostly away from his wife and infant son. He dutifully filed his reports with Washington until he was consigned to a desk job in Foggy Bottom, only a block from both his therapist and his favorite bar.

He paged through the folder, rereading his weekly reports describing the massacres and mutilated bodies discarded by the road like thrown trash from a moving vehicle. He raised a tumbler of Stolikanya to his lips, then knocked the glass on the armrest and sloshed it across his lap.

"Dammit," he said, clumsily brushing his pants leg.

Adele came in from the bath toweling her hair dry. "You said you wouldn't read that stuff anymore."

Henry clutched the file in one hand, not willing to let go. "How can I ignore this?" he said. "They won't even try the sons-of-bitches."

"You need to go to bed," she said.

He sat the glass on the floor and leaned over, ran his hands through his hair. "I'm not tired," he said. His face was elastic and he kneaded it like putty. A bedroom door opened and his son stepped out in his pajamas. "Maurice!" Henry called to him, though he was only steps away. "Son," he said, waving him over. "Come here, come here."

Maurice went reluctantly, knowing how he was. Henry wrapped an arm around him.

"Tell me," he said, "did you read the Nietzsche I gave you? *When you stare into the abyss, the abyss stares back.* Did you know he said that?" He held the boy too hard.

"No, sir," he answered, close enough to smell his father's breath.

"No, you didn't read it, or no, you didn't know he said that? Never mind. Never mind." Henry's forehead dipped and rested on his son's shoulder. "You know all that. I know you do. You just need to read, is all."

Adele stepped in. "That's enough, Henry." She motioned for her son to go and he slipped from his father's grasp.

"Come back here. We need to talk," Henry said. "I saw your sketch book. You're still wasting your time at the foot of a do-nothing God." Henry leaned over and grabbed from the sofa Maurice's copy of *The Prince*. "You read this book," he called to his son. "Every day I want to you to read this book!"

"That's enough, Henry!" Adele cried from the hall, but her husband wouldn't be put down. He threw the book overhand at his son, but in the manner of its fluttering pages it sailed high and struck his wife on the head. Though only a slim volume, its rigid spine found her temple. Adele shrieked and rolled along the wall into the bathroom with a hand pressed to her face. Henry rose from his chair.

Maurice was shaking. "Get away from her!" he screamed. The book lay on the floor between them.

"No, Mauricio," his mother said, angling her face in the mirror. She was composed again and spoke quietly. "Go to bed now. It's okay. Just go to bed."

Maurice relented only after making eye-contact with his mother and seeing she was indeed all right. Henry joined his hands and edged by his son. Before closing his bedroom door, Maurice glanced into the bathroom and saw his father on his knees. His fists made knots in his mother's robe as he buried his face in her belly.

∞

The singing comforted him. The Latin chant and meditative tones dissolved his worries and made sketching easier – a kind of aid to his art. He had been sampling churches all over the city and taking note of their celebrations. Now during the morning service the lady sitting next to him sniffed her disapproval at his sketching during Mass and had no better reaction to the book he carried, but there were no signs at the door saying he couldn't.

It was during communion when he saw her there, his mother, in this solemn procession. Her head was covered by a scarf, and he didn't recognize her until she stood and showed her profile. For a moment he was fearful of being caught, though it was some comfort when he realized he was the one who had caught her.

When Adele Santilli came to the man in the red robes, she raised her chin and opened her mouth. She received the wafer directly on her tongue, then lowered her head and crossed her heart as a return gesture, as if that sealed the deal. Now he understood the ritual as give and take, a kind of exchange of two things of equal value. He studied her as she passed the altar. As she came back to the long bench, Maurice knelt and bowed his head to hide, but was quickly thwarted by his own row of parishioners whose turn it was to stand in the line for the wafer. The indignant old lady next to him shooed him down the row, but when he came to the aisle he broke in the opposite direction.

Once in the sunlight he ran, but was abruptly bound to the piazza by an undetermined thought. Instead of running home, which was his first impulse, he slipped into a narrow street within sight of the church and waited. It was as if he needed to see his mother exiting the church in order to believe he had seen her there at all. A part of him wanted to know she was okay. He felt ashamed. Was his own mother a believer of all his father loathed?

Ten minutes later, amidst the trickle of parishioners, she emerged from the arched doors under the triptych of the last judgement. She untied the scarf and shook out her hair. Then she scanned the piazza and found Maurice's eyes peering from the side of a bakery. He pulled back, but it was too late. She burst around the corner in a playful flourish.

"I won't tell if you won't," she said.

He stared at the hard little shoes she was wearing. "What were you doing in there?"

"Your father and I don't see eye to eye on everything, Mauricio."

"But what were you doing?"

"Celebrating Mass. I guess you didn't know I'm Catholic."

Maurice still wasn't sure what a Catholic was, but if his own mother was one then it couldn't be that bad. He also wondered if by some accident of genetics that he was one too. He stared at the small bruise on her temple. "Does dad know?"

"He knows I was raised in the church. He doesn't know I still go now and then."

"Why do you go there?" Maurice was eager to know if they went for the same reasons. His mother seemed to lose her train of thought, as if confronted with a question she'd never been asked before. "It makes me feel better about things. Life, I suppose."

"Did you go because he hit you with the book last night?"

"No. That was an accident. You have to believe that was an accident. He didn't mean to hurt anyone."

"He was drinking again. He said back home that he stopped."

"I know he did." She pulled him close.

"And nobody said anything this morning. Not a word."

"I'm sorry. We shouldn't have let it go. Your father has seen a lot of bad things in his job. Sometimes he drinks to forget."

"I think he drinks to remember."

Adele stared back at the church where she'd just been absolved. "Maybe I did come here to feel better about last night." Her son touched her forehead by the bluish wound. "It's fine," she said. She motioned toward his sketch pad. "Do you have anything to show me?" He opened the cover and looked uncertain. "Beautiful," she said, leafing through the pages. "But you shouldn't do this during Mass."

"Why not?"

"Mass is celebrated in a special way. You can sketch the altar anytime you want, but Mass is always sacred. It's a special time."

He was let down by her answer. Maurice had a growing problem with regiment, everything dictated, everything prescribed. It seemed contrary to the creative life that was necessary to glorify their God. Artists and builders should be free to worship in their own way when the impulse strikes. He looked to his own unbridled inspiration during Mass, and he considered this force as more organic than religious, a force without barriers.

∞

Maurice came to spend the last hour of the afternoon in his church to practice his new art in silence. He came in quietly and pushed closed the heavy side door near Bramante's cloister. The caretaker had left the door unlocked, as he did each day, and the boy thought he was careful not to let anyone see him slip inside. A light was left on at the front of the nave to light the Raphael fresco he had been working on. Another light glowed from the high altar and its iconic vestige of Mary and her baby. He sat across from the fresco and opened his sketch pad and box of pastels, then laid out several pages of completed studies on the polished marble floor. He might get a larger pad one day and replicate the whole fresco, but for now he was working on two figures at a time, a Sibyl paired with her instructing angel and their bunched up frocks in weightless repose. He started a fresh page under the watchful eyes of the once bleeding Madonna.

The four prophesying Sibyls in the fresco were learning the church's way, but Maurice was learning only Raphael's way of light and color and weightlessness. Every figure was as it should be and no space was left unfinished. He began to understand the spatial idea, but not the intended churchly ideal. He believed deeply in these products of Christ, the oil and tempera and monuments the man had inspired, but Maurice remained remote from Christ himself. Unlike the four Sibyls of Raphael, there were rules he could not learn, ceremonies he could not understand, and traditions too late to instill.

The boy startled when he realized he wasn't alone. Under the side of the dome near the door stood his father. His tie was loose and he stood there looking tired and angry.

"What are you doing here?" his voice echoed.

"I –"

"You need to come home right now." Henry took a few steps forward and saw the pastels on the floor around his son. Then the door creaked open wide and the caretaker hobbled in behind him.

"We are closed! Why you walk in here like the Pope?"

"The last thing I'm trying to do is emulate your Pope," Henry said. "I'm here to get my son."

When the old man noticed the young artist on the floor, he softened his tone. "You may have your son, *Signore*, but you must leave now."

"How did he get in here if the church is closed?"

"I let him do his art," the caretaker said, and then added in Maurice's defense, "he is a good boy."

"And he'll stay a good boy without the likes of all this," he said, mocking the marble walls around him.

Henry turned to see that his son had risen, and in the boy's hand was the book he had made him carry. The night before had hardened him, and seeing his mother in Mass that morning had ignited his own private revolt. Cardinal vices were supplanting the virtues. Stone had become Maurice's God, like books had become the gods of his father. So with some residual memory of the night before, he raised his arm and took aim at his father, aimed for his head that was staring back now in bewilderment. Once in motion the boy spoke to his God and God spoke back. His sight rose to the high altar as the words of the dead philosopher left his hand. With Henry taking cover and the confused caretaker looking on, the book sailed high toward the miracle mother of God. In equal amounts of doubt and hope, Maurice waited to see if words would make her bleed.

Raw Toscana

THE COMMUNIST PARTY sought friends and converts by way of the belly, throwing a village festival with an arousing penne and cream sauce. As I gorged on the slippery pasta and nursed a carafe of Chianti at one of the long tables striping the piazza, I ran a fork through the warm cheeses like a palette knife on canvas, and thought for a moment I could paint with it. I imagined an edible painting, a canvas of Biscotti and pigments of local cuisine, mixed live and served from the menu – pomodoro reds and cappuccino ochers.

"How did you end up in Travenelle?" the Brit across the table asked, jolting me back to reality. His mouth was full of roasted chicken and his teeth beamed through the debris like a strand of greasy pearls.

"Just a stopover," I said. "I'm trying to get to Siena."

"Going for the *Running of the Bulls*?"

"That's Pamplona, Simon," his wife said. "In Siena it's *The Palio*; the horse race."

"Ah, yes. Horses running in circles. That should be a fine spectacle."

His wife, Audrey, had a round and pretty face, but she lacked Simon's dental fortune.

"Did you notice the plates at breakfast this morning?" I asked. "The placement of the knife and croissant made an abstract hammer and sickle."

"Could be worse. They could have been swastikas," said Simon. "Don't worry about our hosts, Michael. Italian politics is secondary to Italian pleasure. Food, wine, and opera rank much higher. Take the chefs, for instance." At the high end of the piazza, two of the town's finest chefs were squabbling over an open stove, flailing their ladles as if conducting opposing orchestras.

"We all have our priorities," I said, as I wiped up the last of my imaginary paint with a tuft of bread. Audrey raised her hand to order another carafe as my eye caught our new waitress. My first impression, among many, was of her lengths. Her black silk hair, fingernails, and eyelashes were all longer than vogue. Dark hairs hatched her arms in fine brush strokes, and her legs stretched and arched like a black widow in a web. Her attention passed over Audrey's hand and locked into my eyes. She pursed her lips and mouthed *vino rosso?*

"*Per favore*," I said, wiping a spittle of white sauce from my lips. She turned away, and I watched her legs fade into the dark of the restaurant.

"You'll enjoy Siena," said Simon. "They're more democratic."

"I'm not going there for the democracy."

"Ah, the horse race."

"Actually, no. That'll just be a distraction. I'm going there for the color." I craned my neck for the waitress.

"The color?"

"I want to understand brown." And I did. If I could master a palate of nothing but browns, then I could work into the primaries with confidence. It was my way of getting back to basics.

"I suppose Siena would be a logical place to study brown. Have you toured Umbria?"

"I'd like to, but I'm running out of time. I've been touring hill towns for the past month. I paint."

Angelica, our new barmaid, was coming our way with two carafes of red wine. I was trying to behave myself, but she didn't make it easy. I couldn't decide if her blouse was half open or half buttoned.

"*Due?*" I said, catching her olive eyes. "You're trying to get us drunk?"

"*Uno per il signore inglese e sua moglie, e uno per il bell'Americano.*" She wrapped her hand around the nape of my neck as she poured my glass full.

"You want the translation, Michael?" Audrey asked. "She's trying to get you shit-faced." She raised her empty glass to be filled, but had lost her cheer at my flirtation with Angelica. I had met Simon and Audrey at the hotel that morning as our rooms were being prepared, and since we had hit it off we decided to spend the day together. Though I didn't know her, I sensed in her a heightened gleefulness that afternoon, and as best I could tell, it had something to do with being escorted through the ancient Tuscan streets with a man on each arm.

Angelica kept her hand on my neck as she poured Audrey's glass.

"I no get people drunk. People get themselves drunk, no?"

She was beautiful and she was getting me drunk, but not on wine.

"Your English is good," I said to her.

"Yes," she said, nodding across the table toward Simon and Audrey. "They are very nice."

I was tempted to steer her into my lap when a boisterous table of graying Italians, probably communists, summoned her away to help, as Angelica put it, get themselves drunk.

"I think she's smitten with you, Michael. I know that look. I get it from Audrey every day." Simon patronized his wife's hand with a little squeeze.

"My look isn't quite that trashy." She raised her glass, then turned to me and said, "We'll be your chaperones for the evening, Michael. I'll make a complete report to your lovely Catherine in the morning."

I had left Catherine, my fiancée, in her air-conditioned suite in Paris. Her pink skin wasn't suited for the sun of the Italian peninsula, she had declared. Autumn was barely tolerable. She seemed more suited to spending her summers in the cool boutiques along the Boulevard de la Madeleine, spending her father's money.

"I've been faithful to Catherine since the day we met," I said, and it was true, though I didn't disclaim we'd known each other for only six months. After all that Catherine had done for me, I owed her my fidelity, which was admittedly something I had never given anyone. I guess this trip was the first test. 'Go,' she had said to me, 'take the month and paint and find your brown.' It was like she was sending me on a shopping trip to pick up some inspiration.

The ancient town hall cast its final shadow over the stone palazzo behind us, and the sky dimmed to a deep ultramarine, punctuated only by the glowing dime of a rising moon. The two chefs sat together now, reconciled over a bottle of grappa, and the piazza buzzed with storytelling and bits of local gossip. One area of tables was being cleared for dancing, and a local rock band began setting up their equipment.

Simon glanced over my shoulder. "I don't know if this is the warm-up act or the intermission, Michael, but I believe they're burning your flag."

I turned around to see a hapless mob of ornery Italians in a huddle. The same portly gentleman who had taken my credit card at the hotel struck the match. Earlier he had referred to me as his "American friend."

"That's the hotel guy," I said.

"He is Antonio," said a German gentleman with a Lenin tipped beard sitting down from Simon. "He owns half the town. Many business interests in Travenelle."

"So he's a hotelier, a real estate baron, and heads the local polit bureau," I said. "I bet he sells flags too." I felt a familiar hand in my hair and turned my head near Angelica's breast.

"No worry about Papa," she said, dismissively. "He is consumed with old ways, but I am not Communist. I am Italian. Let me fill your glass."

And I believed her. Political affiliation didn't matter in her presence.

"You a big time capitalist, no? Big shot Americano with a big . . . eh . . . *portafoglio*." She waved her palm, searching. "Wallet?"

"The only things I sell are my paintings. I am an artist." But not many recently. Just enough to pay for canvas and paint and the lousiest pensions. I was doing okay up to a year ago, but it didn't last. In another six months I was starving.

"*Un artista!*"

Her whole body moved when she said that word. She could have said the Italian word for 'bowling ball,' and I would have crumbled like an old fresco. My fiancée's father, sitting behind his hand-carved desk, had said the same word at our introduction, but in an entirely different way.

The official protest concluded with the stars and stripes frittering to ash, and the rock band kicked into their first tune, some overplayed U2 cover. We were each into our third liter of wine, and everyone in the piazza seemed closer and louder as we all leaned in and talked over the band.

"You came here through Poggibonsi? *We* came through Poggibonsi!" said Simon, looking for an excuse to celebrate. "Tell me, how in bloody hell could anyone name a place Poggibonsi?" He turned to his wife. "Pardon me love, I was going to step out and I was wondering if you needed me to pick up anything in Poggibonsi?" We pounded our fists on the table and laughed until our bladders hurt. Several empty glasses fell over in the clatter. Simon motioned over my shoulder. "I think we're going to receive a guest." Antonio, the communist innkeeper, was barreling toward us with his belly clearing the way.

"*Benvenuti*, my American friends!" his voice boomed over the band. "I am so happy you have come. Welcome to *Unita'Festival*!"

"The two of us are from England," Audrey said, mustering a little dead empire pride.

"No matter. Welcome. I hope you have not taken our fun too seriously. We are family first. Politics come second."

"We've enjoyed it." I said. "The food especially."

"When our chefs fight, we know we will eat well," he said, before pointing a fat finger at my chest. "But I know what *you* enjoy. I see things with my eyes. My daughter rebels, or she thinks she rebels. She eyes you." His cheeks plumped as he smiled. "She thinks I will not approve, but no, I worry for you. She is trouble enough for Italian blood, but you, you will be eaten alive!"

This felt like a challenge I couldn't refuse, but I wasn't showing my hand. I held up my palms, shook my head. "I'm just here to enjoy the food and company."

"And our women, and that is no fault. I went to America once, to New York to visit my brother. He lives in . . . in Satin Island, you know? I eat your food, drink your drink, fuck your women. Makes for very pleasure and good time. So you in Travenelle, you do as Travenelles do, no?"

I played along, laughing with Antonio and his belly full of Chianti.

"*Benissimo*. You laugh good. A man must laugh to enjoy life. You take my daughter with laughter, you may survive." He made a sweeping gesture with his hand. "I see the future. My grandson will be half communist and half capitalist. Bread for lunch and circus for dinner." He gave a joyous guttural sound and slapped my back entirely too hard as he danced back to his table. As I stared helplessly at the red wine stain in my lap, Angelica reappeared from the shadows with a towel and dabbed my pants in long slow strokes.

Simon leaned over his glass. "*Scusi*, uh . . . Angelica, I believe it is. Have you by chance found Poggibonsi down there?" Audrey grabbed Simon, who was giggling hysterically, and dragged him into the throng of dancers. I stuck my face in Angelica's hair.

"Let me paint you."

"*Sì*, of course."

"Tomorrow. We'll start in the morning and hike into the hills. I want to see you in the Tuscan sun."

"I will bring a lunch."

"Dance with me."

"I must work."

"You're killing me."

"Tomorrow," she said, pressing two long fingers over my lips. She brushed her hand over my cheek as she walked away.

I watched Simon and Audrey dance badly until they stumbled back to the table and fell into their chairs like sacks of oats. Simon immediately rose and excused himself to find a toilet, mocking a goose-step on the way. Audrey drained the last drop from a carafe, then swirled her glass and stared at my chest as though she were a man and I had breasts.

"I know what you're up to, you and your beer-tending amante with the long legs. You Americans ever heard of fidelity?"

"I've done nothing but a little innocent flirting. Nothing less than what we've been doing all day." This seemed to catch her off-guard.

"Flirting? You Americans are all alike. So self-centered. We just thought you might be lonely and wanted company." She tossed her hair aside and turned to the band.

"Oh come on, Audrey. We've been playing all day," I countered, but she didn't respond as her eyes were glazing over from the wine.

Simon stumbled back to the table and suggested turning in for the evening. I flagged the other waitresses, asking each where Angelica had gone, but no one claimed any knowledge. The three of us eventually wound our way through the streets to the hotel, at one point breaking into an off-key mocking tribute to the band.

We fell into the hotel lobby and called for our room keys. A barrel of a man lumbered toward us and slapped our keys on the counter, then retreated to a back room and the harking blue glow of a television.

"Time to tinkle, love." Audrey meandered toward the end of the hall to the common bath for the floor.

Simon fiddled with the key in his lock. "Audrey and I are going hiking in the morning, in case you'd like to join us."

"No, thanks. I've made plans."

"Going to find your brown?"

"Something like that." He didn't take my pursuit too seriously. I knew if I could capture the subtleties of brown, then I could work back into color and keep my palate under control. So much is about control.

After trying several doors, I found my room, stripped, and sunk into my mattress about six feet. In what could have been anywhere from five minutes to an hour, there was a knock at the door. I climbed out of bed as if escaping from a net.

"What?" I said, squinting from the dim bulb in the hall.

"Is Audrey with you, Michael? Is she here?" Simon stood in the doorway with his shirt half tucked in.

"No," I wondered aloud, as if the question was presented in a dream. "We were just flirting. No. Wait . . . why would she be here?"

"She's not back from the toilet. She seems to have wandered off."

"I'm sure she's fine."

"It's not like her. It's not."

I was being enlisted for a search party. By the time I was dressed, Simon was in the street calling Audrey's name into dark corners as if he'd find her in a doorway suckling a bottle.

"I'll take the alleys behind the hotel," I said. "You take the street back to the festival." He agreed and I slid into a narrow passage. The stone walls were lit by a moonbeam sliver of sky, and I wondered how the light would have fallen on Angelica's skin. The alley opened into a small cortile with a lone olive tree glowing in the far corner. Under the tree was a nicely shaped ass heaving up and down, and when it settled onto a pair of plump ankles, Audrey showed her face and mine drew a smile.

"Too good to throw-up in a squat toilet? You British are all alike."

"Fuck you."

"Can I help you up?"

"I can manage just fine. I feel better now."

"Simon's looking for you. He's worried."

"Simon worries too much." She stumbled as she tried to stand, and I caught her, then we both stumbled and held each other up. "I can manage myself," she said.

We held each other for an awkward moment, and then she kissed me. It was long and soft and of the lips only, until I lost myself and thrust my tongue and found the bitters of bile between her teeth. I drew back and stiffened. She raised her hand to my chest and pushed me away.

"Go back to your fiancée, Michael."

She left me alone in the courtyard under the olive tree, its leaves shivering light and silver.

∞

Cool air blew through the shutters and sprayed the room with bright stripes of morning light. I peeled my eyes open and separated the pounding in my head with the gentle knock on the door.

"*Buon Giorno*, Michael," Angelica cooed as if waking a child.

"Morning . . . giorno." I wrapped both hands around my forehead.

"We meet at noon? In lobby?"

"I'll be there."

Her response was muffled and I heard her footsteps echo down the hall.

I struggled out of bed and sat on a chair by my open suitcase. Shirts and underwear were spilling onto the floor, and a lone sock reached out to one side, searching for its mate. I grabbed my wallet and pulled out a photo of Catherine and rubbed its edge with my thumb. She had been a savior of sorts. When I met her I was in the artists' death trap of painting the same scene over and over; the one that always sold, though never for much money. I wasn't even cleaning my palette. Little craters of dried paint melted into one another, all competing for space. I was afraid to lose the formula.

Catherine found me in a café in Lyon. I don't know what did it for her; my desperation, my poverty, or my salvageable looks. She watched me down an espresso in one shot and came over to remind me that it's not good to look too American these days. Then she offered to buy me another espresso and teach me the finer points of what to do with it. Who was I to refuse?

She lived with her father in Paris where he made gobs of euro in import-export. Given his taste, it was probably in exporting American pop shit to every quaint postcard hamlet on the planet. As an ice-breaker, I gave him the last of my formula paintings, which could have housed and fed me for another week. Being a detail man, he examined it as though it was a blueprint of every intangible molecule of my being, then stuck it in his filing cabinet where he had probably already started a dossier.

He tried to warn Catherine off, which made it all the more surprising when he finally agreed to help me. Catherine got her way; she loved me, or so she said, and she loved my portfolio of paintings that I couldn't seem to paint anymore. Which she loved more, I don't know. Part of me thought it was my starving artist appeal. She had this pretentious notion of uncovering a great talent and nurturing him to stardom. Nurturing to Catherine meant dressing me in nice clothes and showing me off to her theatre friends. I guess sometimes we all need someone to save, and at the time, I needed saving. We were engaged two months later.

After breakfast I primed a canvas, preparing the surface to take Angelica's flesh. All I remembered from the night before was a residue of insane lust I had for her under the influence. Her face I'd already forgotten, her figure a dream. I reduced her to a still life of baskets and fruit, waiting to be arranged and composed. I had a model for the day, just a model, and for that I was grateful.

Angelica greeted me wearing a sundress of flowering orchids that hung lightly over her shoulders, giving her the curves of a gently blowing sheer. Lean viridian cypress lined the road out of town, and we walked under their pointy shadows until Angelica turned us through an ancient gate under a siege of vines. We passed into a meadow of sunbaked grasses, and from there ran endless vineyards, fences of green, and furrows bending with the earth. The vines, full of embryonic grapes the size of peas, dangled lightly on their crosses.

"Come," she said. "I know a place."

She led me up a hill between the lines of trellis and I stumbled along behind her, trying to keep the boney legs of my easel from brushing the virgin vines. We came to a small patch of grass, an island in a sea of ripening fruit, and I raised my easel and Angelica her blanket.

"First, we eat," she said, and began laying out rolls of *proscuitto* and little cubes of provolone. I sat on the far edge of the blanket and watched her slender hands do their work.

"I like your shirt, Michael. You must be very successful artist to afford such clothes."

"I have someone who picks out my wardrobe," I said. "Here, let me." I took the bottle of red and raised its cork, selling myself the idea that its contents would cleanse the residue in my head from the night before. I saturated my mouth with the first sweet sip, and, after resisting the gag reflex, remembered the last time I saw her.

"Where did you go after I finished dinner? I looked for you."

"I tell you. I had to work."

"But you were working there."

She sliced off a section of bread like she was decapitating a small animal.

"Papa has many businesses."

"And you work for Papa?"

"Si. I work for Papa."

She lost her smile. I was afraid I had pried too much. The sun reached its post-noon swelter and a moist film had formed over her body, making her appear well oiled. I was beginning to sweat.

"We should get started," I said. I left her on the woolen stage and took my place behind the easel where I laid out my paints, an ode to brown, with yellow and beige fingers to draw out the palette. With a stick of charcoal in hand, I looked from behind the easel in time to see Angelica's dress float to the ground. Her bare skin was cut from a bolt of satin of some exotic Mediterranean hue. She stood statuesque, hands on hips; all oil, body and curve.

"How would you like me?"

"Ah . . . umm. Sit down and turn your torso like . . . like that. Good. That's wonderful." As quickly as I was overcome with her beauty, I overcame a whimsical urge to bang my head into the canvas. I took another sip of wine, a large sip, and began sketching, working the charcoal gently at first, then picking up attitude. This wasn't to be another formula painting. A lone black line traced her thigh and faded in. One oblong circle hung a breast, and a soft point made the other in profile. Sweeps of brown paint were next, folds and creases and narrow places touched and patterned by fingers of bristles. I made her in abstraction and made her my own, and she didn't even know it.

I wanted to paint this for Catherine, for the things she had done for me. I wanted it to rise above formula, to peel away the layers of the subject, not just let the eyes speak, but fill the nose and shoulders with voice, give each bump and knuckle a story. While watching my hand move free I realized that control was a bastard. I stripped away the layers of safety and let the brush love the canvas.

A half hour passed and I was soaked with sweat and coming down off my first burn. The process was sound, and I was invigorated, frustrated, and alive. Angelica was ready for a break.

"How much longer?" she asked.

"Okay. Take a break."

She stretched and arched her back, drawing her breasts taut and parting her legs. I struggled to find a neutral subject.

"When will the grapes be ready?" I asked.

"No, no. The grapes are not ready. The grapes will not be ready for some time."

"You can't rush art, eh?" I sat down, again on the far side of the blanket and tried to focus on the pea-size grapes. Together, Angelica and I made a sort of Manet picnic.

"No. We must not rush art. The greater the art, the greater the riches," she said, running her fingers through her hair. "What is wrong, Michael? Are you well?"

"I'm fine. I'm thinking about my process. My colors."

"What is wrong with your colors?" She crawled across the blanket, her breasts and hair swaying, and sat by my side.

"I'm not sure. I'm not mixing right."

"I think we mix well."

"That's not what I mean."

"I think your colors are *belli*," she said, taking the brush from my hand. "Do you have a color for this?" She ran the bristles over her skin, painting a waning half-moon around her areola. I traced the other half-moon with my finger and cupped her.

There is a place on the undersides of eyelids where all colors merge in a sparkling prism. In this field-view lies every color simultaneously in a kind of coop that transcends all prejudice and all jealousy. Everything is equal and everything is fair. We tangled between the vines in this color prism, and I found my brown and tasted its salt in full color. After release, we lay on our backs and slept between the sun and the rolling bonsai hills.

I woke to see her bending over her basket, her knobby spine trailing down to her breezeway. She stood and dropped her dress over her shoulders, then flung her hair from side to side. She corked the wine bottle and tossed it in her basket.

"Did I do something wrong?" I asked.

"No. You are well," she said blankly.

"I still wanted to have another hour with you and the canvas."

"Perhaps another time."

"Tomorrow?" I grabbed my underwear.

"That is up to Papa."

"Ask Papa for the day off. I want to see you. I *need* to see you."

"I go now, Michael."

"Can I see you tonight?"

"No. I work."

Antonio was right, she was difficult. I summoned my will and took her hand, but she pulled away with a loathsome eye. She snapped up the blanket, folding it in three quick wisps. Under her arm it went, and with the basket in hand she left our garden and descended the hill, the vineyard slowly swallowing her figure.

I went back to the canvas to see *my* Angelica, disjointed and mysterious, lengths out of proportion. There was an underside to her, a depth I hadn't felt in the flesh, but exposed under my brush. She was seductive and horrible, and I'd never painted anything like it. I had to finish it, but for the moment I couldn't touch it. I stood there staring into the canvas until I heard a rustling from up the hill.

"Look, Audrey. This must be one of those nude artist colonies we read about."

My clothes were scattered as if tossed by a storm. I just stood there in my boxers.

"I've heard of painting nudes, Michael, but really." Audrey came to my side, taking care not to touch me, and stared into Angelica's abstraction. She knew.

"For your lovely Catherine's sake, I hope it's finished."

"No painting is ever finished." I grabbed my pants and wrestled them on.

"She obviously wasn't as much trouble as her father said."

Simon looked the painting over and pulled Audrey to his side. "Love, all this sudden nakedness has made me a bit raw. May I escort you back to our hotel room?" Audrey rocked in her husband's arms, then took his hand and led him down Angelica's path.

Before they bobbed out of site, Audrey called over her shoulder, "Your art is inspiring, Michael!"

That evening I went to all five restaurants in town. Each maître d' offered me a table, and each time I refused more rudely than I intended.

"Do you know her? Do you know where she's working tonight?"

Even the ones I knew who spoke English pretended not to, and they cloaked themselves in innocent smiles and offered me tourist menus with unbelievable pictures of each dish.

At the last restaurant I spotted Simon and Audrey nestled in back at a table for two, gazing into each other's eyes and balancing each other. I waved to them like I had just run into old friends, but Audrey distracted herself, took Simon's hand, and leaned in close. I heard Simon's cackle all the way to the street, where the first drops of rain were pelting the canvas awning.

I stepped out into the piazza and felt the cold piercing drops of rain slice through the lingering heat of the day. I wound my way to the hotel, summoning my nerve.

"I need to speak with Antonio."

The night auditor didn't answer. Just as he did the night before, he dropped my key on the counter and lumbered back to his program.

In my room the sound of rain made the walls soft and the floors hard, and I uncovered my Angelica and sat her under the light. Catherine will still be excited, I thought. She couldn't help but to be excited. Looking into that painting was like looking into a mirror and seeing your eye had changed color. There were new layers I had never found under my brush, all with an urgency that didn't exist a day before. Then I realized, even without another sitting, I had uncovered a new layer of my art. Angelica could disappear. Everyone could disappear. I was out of my slump.

∞

The next morning I stood in the hotel lobby with the train schedule in my hand, the Florence-to-Paris lines circled, waiting to check out. Antonio slid the bill across the cold travertine counter, then pretended to read something important from a stack of papers on his desk. I perused the bill.

"300 euro for 'special services?' What the hell is this? The room was only 60 euro."

Antonio peered over his frame glasses, his eyes different. "I am afraid you have lost your humor, my friend. Perhaps the mistake is yours?"

"I don't think so."

Antonio transformed from the jovial clown at the festival to a bull moose posture, his formerly unthreatening gut now an impenetrable rampart.

"*Un momento, Signore*. This is not your credit card. The name does not match your passport. I cannot stand by while you make a fraud on me." He grabbed the telephone.

"It's my father-in-law's card. My future father-in-law."

"Ah. Then I will be happy to detail the charges to your future father-in-law."

"That won't be necessary. What the hell are the charges?"

The door behind me creaked open, and Angelica swept into the lobby and passed behind the counter wearing the same flowering orchids from the day before. She opened a cabinet drawer and deposited a roll of bills.

"*Buon Giorno, bella mia*," her father cooed.

"*Buon Giorno, papa*."

Her eyes swept over me as if they might whisk me onto the street before she disappeared into the back room and slammed the door.

"She models for you, no?" Antonio said. "And other services?"

I couldn't look into his eyes. For a moment I said nothing, as if waiting for divine intervention. Then I raised my head in desperation, "I'd appreciate it if you would leave the bill as vague as possible."

"For a mere ten euro, cash, *Signore*, I will be happy to process the bill with a minimum of detail."

I dug into my wallet and pulled out the last of the cash Catherine had given me and slid it across the counter. Antonio tore up the itemized bill and wrote a new one with only a total room charge at the bottom. As I signed the receipt, I predicted I would suffer the least consequence with one extravagant hotel stay.

"But of course," Antonio said, "if contacted by the card holder, I will have to detail the charges. It is business, you understand?"

I threw the pen on the counter. "I thought we reached an agreement?"

The night auditor stepped out of the back room and stood behind Antonio, his arms folded.

"*Signore*," he said gravely. "You have lost your humor. You do not want to lose anything else."

I gathered my suitcase, easel, and portfolio, and stumbled out the door into the street. The earlier showers made the stone pavers glisten, and I stood there squinting and disoriented before finding my bearing to the bus station.

I sat outside at the station trattoria and ordered an American coffee. My portfolio leaned against the next table, bulging with abandoned work, and I pulled it toward me and unzipped it for another look at Angelica's image. There were lines of fear I hadn't seen before. The browns fought in chaotic clashes and textures of conflict, as if she was trapped and trying to get out of her skin. It was raw and unknown, and it worked, and it was a part of me. I zipped up the portfolio and kept it close to my side.

As I finished my coffee, I noticed a charred piece of blue fabric with the tip of a star at my feet. I imagined it pointing north, toward Catherine. The bus to Florence was due in an hour, and from Florence, the train to Paris. Catherine's father would be interested in the progress of my work, and of course, the details of my travels.

The bus south to the hills of Poggibonsi was due in five minutes. From there I could catch the train to Siena and fade into Umbria. There I could disappear into my art. My compass spun. North and south stood off in my head like two chefs arguing over how best to proceed, for the sake of taste and direction and control.

At the end of the narrow street the sun flashed a glimmer of light off a windshield, and a bus roared into view, spewing the damp morning air with diesel. It coughed to a stop as the doors swung open, wide and inviting. The sign in the front window was torn in half and just said "*bonsi.*" I gathered my things, checked for my wallet, and boarded the bus.

Skating the Blumlisalp

WE HAD SOME SUSPICION when we saw him at the pre-climb prep meeting. One hundred and ten pounds of body matter shrink-wrapped to the bones, and a skeletal head teetering on his shoulders as though attached by a gimbal. I took him for being mildly retarded before I even heard his speech impediment. The liberal minded were afraid for him; the conservatives were afraid for themselves.

"This Terry guy is going?" Rick said. "No way. I'll end carrying his ass halfway up the mountain and down again."

Rick was my best friend, or at least the best I had at the time. He did everything full speed, always, and hated anything that slowed him down. Summer vacation to Rick was no more than a break between baseball season and football practice.

I shook my head. "Doesn't look good, does it?" And it didn't. We were going for the postcard view, a three thousand meter pass, but this guy didn't seem up to the task.

Terry stood and walked stiffly, and spoke little, as though a stiffness in his jaw prevented him.

"You two hush. He'll hear you," Jill whispered. "Let's just be there for him and encourage him. I think it's wonderful." We had met her in the hotel bar in Zurich a week before, and I invited her to join us on the hike. She was a little thing with stringy blond hair and an oily face; certainly worth pursuing, but she would have been more attractive if she applied herself.

Yoyo, our guide, didn't seem concerned about Terry. He sized up our group with one glance, then motioned for Terry to sit by his side. The remaining eight of us gathered around them like disciples as we poured over a contour map.

The next day we set off from Kandersteg, southwest of Interlaken. As the sun rose, the morning grew darker as a cold front blew over and filled the valley with sullen grey clouds.

Rick, undaunted and in full bravado, charged up the first leg, a rutted jeep trail, sometimes outpacing Yoyo. Terry brought up the rear, as expected, slowly and mechanically with little pigeon steps, and Jill and I hovered in the middle. Since the clouds were descending, I kept behind Jill thinking she might provide the best view. Everyone kept glancing over their shoulders to see if Terry was still with us. Jill marveled at his every step.

"You're doing so well, Terry. But it's going to get a lot harder as we go," Jill said as she adjusted her new Swiss climbing hat with the tips of her fingers. "If you need us to slow down, you just yell."

Rick looked back and smirked. Terry didn't seem to hear her, and I was beginning to think he was deaf on top of the rest of his oddities. The only time he looked up was at the distant rumble of some unseen airplane.

At the end of the first leg we rested by a mountain lake plateau, capped by a second plateau of dense cloud. Beyond the ice-grey lake I could only imagine what we were climbing in to. Terry or no Terry, our postcard view wasn't happening.

We began the second leg at the lakeshore where the mountain face was the steepest. The trail clung to the cliff face, and we watched the lake fall below our feet with each step. As we cleared the lake, the slopes opened up and the trail splintered into a myriad of gouges, where we each choose a separate path to find our way. Rick favored large steps and great strides, mounting stones like a conqueror. Jill fancied the trails as more of a maze, choosing a wandering path that might capture the most experience. Terry stepped as straight as possible, from point A to point B, carefully, so as not to disturb the grass or lichen.

As the trees thinned and fell behind, the trails merged into one and we entered the cloud. The grass reduced itself to one length, like thick moss, and rock out-crops scattered like litter. We gathered on a small ledge for lunch and were quickly surrounded by a shepardless herd of goats adding their bells to the air.

I planted myself on a rock and pulled several wool sweaters from my pack. It was sixty-five degrees in the valley, but forty-five degrees on my rock. I made the mistake of wearing a cotton T-shirt, and it clung to my body like a cold wet rag. I layered up and sneezed three times.

Terry was the last to arrive. He stood alone, his pack sagging from his bony shoulders, staring through the cloud as though into the dramatic view we were hoping for. He soaked in the haze for a minute, then sat his pack on a large stone and carefully removed his extra layers as if retrieving fine linen from an open drawer. Each jacket and wool sweater was folded perfectly. He layered himself and took a sandwich back to the non-view, chewing and chewing as though he forgot how to swallow.

I turned to Rick. "I noticed you limping a little. How's that knee holding up?"

He was bent over, wrapping a shirt around his left knee. His belongings spilled out of his pack onto the ground. "I had it rehabbed pretty well last winter, but it feels a little tight. Nothing to hold me back though." He stood and grinned wide. "You get a load of Terry? Dude walks like he has a stick up his ass."

A small stone flew over Rick's head from Jill's direction.

"He can't hear me," Rick said, and turned back to me. "Damn girl is dangerous."

Jill scowled as she peeled off her new boots. Each tongue had licked around an ankle, and blisters pocketed on every knob of her feet.

"He's doing just fine," she said, stretching a bony white toe.

"He's been dragging his tail the whole way, and we haven't even hit the hard part yet."

Terry was off to one side chewing his sandwich. Yoyo was attempting a conversation with him, but the awkward little man offered little more than two word sentences and a few facial quirks. His thin frame was bundled in sweaters, and he stood there intent on the clouds, a mathematician in shoulder pads lost in some equation.

In a half hour the group was humming again. I extended my hand to Jill, and she took it as I pulled her to her feet and helped with her pack. The group set out on a strong pace, but the gradient increased, moon-rock quickly spread out above them, and ten people with ten competing metabolisms gave way to a slow, inconsistent march. The line resembled a Slinky, expanding on each advance and contracting at each rest. We stopped whenever Terry fell out of sight in the fog.

Energy came in bursts and faded with each step. All my joints compressed as I focused my eyes on the spot where my next boot would fall. To mask the pain I played songs in my head, taking steps to the beat. I wondered what everyone was doing to handle the fatigue. I looked back to Rick, who had steadily given up position. I could tell by his face alone that his knee was worse, but now his limp was accompanied by a barely audible grunt.

"You okay back there?" I called.

Lines strained from each corner of his mouth. "Yeah . . . yeah," he said with each step. Terry was right behind him, walking the same way he had walked into the prep meeting the day before.

For two more hours we advanced in Terry-size steps and small rests when Yoyo called back through the fog, "We made it!" After another few painful strides I joined Yoyo on a flat stone terrace, where we stood in triumph as though we had discovered some ancient ruin. The pad was for the supply helicopter. The Alpine *hutte* was just above us, camouflaged in mist and native stone; only the red striped Swiss shutters setting it off.

"It is customary to congratulate each other at the top of a climb." Yoyo grabbed my hand and shook it vigorously, then stepped past me and embraced Jill as she took her last step. Rick had dropped to the end of the line, his face scowling, but with the goal in sight he had a rush of adrenaline. He thrust past Terry, nearly knocking him off the mountain, before reaching the landing pad. I was surprised he didn't yell "touchdown!"

We all gave hi-fives and cheap hugs, and massaged our egos. It was a good excuse to hug Jill and I held on a little longer than I should have, but she didn't seem to mind. For those few minutes on the stone terrace in the cloud, the lack of view didn't seem to matter. Terry stood among us without expression, erect as a pencil, shaking everyone's hand like he was in a receiving line. He wasn't even out of breath.

∞

"So, how you feeling, Terry?" Rick said as he swaggered to the oak table.

"Sore."

"Sore, eh? Well, it was a hell of a climb. You *should* be sore. You did good, little man." Rick pivoted heavily on his right leg and sat beside me. He whispered, "I just hope he can get his ass down." Jill sat across from me wincing, and Terry next to her. Jill and I warmed our hands around enormous bowls of steaming coffee. Rick slapped his palms on the edge of the table and leaned his nose forward. "Well looky here. Terry likes to draw airplanes. That's pretty good."

"Leave him alone, Rick," Jill said.

"What? I said it was good."

"Those are beautiful Terry. Where did you learn to draw like that?"

"School."

"That's wonderful. Good for you. So you like to study art? Are you going to be an artist?"

"No. Engineer." His frail hand kept working the pencil lead, giving depth to the wings.

"Oh, you're going to drive trains! Wouldn't that be wonderful?" Jill looked like she had the urge to reach over and touch him. Terry didn't answer. Rick rolled his eyes, and I sneezed.

"*Gesundheit*," Jill said. "You're not looking too good." She touched my forehead instead, then dropped her hand to mine.

"Got a chill on the way up," I said. "I wore a cotton tee. Should have known better."

"Yoyo told you about that at the prep meeting," Rick said. "He also told you about the altitude. Jill, did you hear what happened?"

"Rick," I said irritably.

"The master climber over here got up from his nap before dinner and passed out. You should have seen his eyes roll back into his head," Rick said, tracing his fingers over the graffiti carved in the table.

"It was just the oxygen," I said to Jill. "I got up too fast. So how about you? How are your feet?"

"Not real good. I have blisters on both feet and they're all on fire." She warmed her face over the bowl of coffee. "To tell you the truth, I'm dreading tomorrow."

"It's eight hours to the funicular. I'm afraid you don't have much choice."

"Thanks a lot, but neither do you." She glared at Rick. "And neither do you! Is your knee going to hold up or are we going to have to get Terry to carry you down?"

"My knee is freshly wrapped and doing just fine, thank you." Rick was always a good liar. Terry abandoned his drawings and said goodnight. He mouse-stepped to the bunk room. "Doesn't have much to say, does he?"

∞

The bunks slept two dozen per room in one long bed; twelve on top and twelve on the bottom, all co-ed. We each claimed a blanket and waited for the room to quiet down, which amounted to several hours of people fumbling about and waiting for the Swedes in the top bunk to finish screwing.

"Pretty cool drawings," Rick said, lying beside me with his hands cradling his head. "You know, I've heard about stuff like that. Stupid people being talented in art and stuff. Shit you wouldn't expect."

"Yeah, he's real good." I said, before tuning him out.

Jill was on my other side and we rolled into each other, interlocking arms and legs. As we weren't as bold as the Swedes, I kept to her lips and dreamed of being in a room with twenty-two less people. But then, in true European fashion, and in spite of sharing a bed with such a multitude, my hand started wandering over Jill's chest, sifting under her clothes like I was breaking through the clouds. Her moan went unnoticed, slid between the various snores in the room. Then one particular snore rose above the rest. It wasn't a sound from the throat, but was a moist smacking of the tongue and lips like a dog drinking water from a dish; the pitch rising higher on inhalation and falling bitterly on the exhale. I was transported back to the room of sweaty hikers.

I untangled myself from Jill, leaned up, and looked down the line of bodies for the culprit. It was Terry laying in dead man's pose with his mouth churning like he was still chewing his sandwich.

Rick sat up. "Jesus, man. Do you believe this? It sounds like someone's getting a huge hummer down there." I nudged Rick, and he reached over two other bodies and punched Terry on the shoulder. "Buddy. Quiet down!" Terry went from chewing his sandwich to chewing gum, his mouth now partially closed.

"Thanks Rick," I said. "I knew I brought you along for something."

"That was rude! Both of you!" Jill rolled over, practically into another room, and wrapped the blanket around her. I touched her shoulder and felt her recoil.

Lying on my back, staring at the bottom of the Swede's satisfied bunk, I tried to shift my thoughts to the second leg of the hike, but all I saw was a disheartening haze. At least Terry was quiet – for about two minutes.

"Fuck," Rick said.

There was a rustling at the other end of the bunk where the English slept. "Bloody hell. Will one of you blokes either kiss him or roll him over?"

∞

"Oh man. You gotta see this."

I squinted and remembered where I was. Rick stood at the end of the bunk staring out the window with his matted hair in silhouette. Jill was already gone. I kicked off the blanket, jumped up, and fell immediately onto the floor in a pathetic lump. Waiting for my vision to return, I tried to reconcile my sobriety with the black-out drunk vacancy in my head.

"Breathe man, breathe. Do I have to keep telling you?"

"I'm fine. Give me a minute."

"It's like training your dog, but your dog learns." Rick shuffled off to breakfast with a noticeable limp.

I sat up cross-legged, did a little deep breathing, and opened my eyes unusually wide several times. My sinuses felt like they were filled with concrete. Holding onto the bunk post, I pulled myself up to the window.

The sky was a blue I couldn't name; one I have only seen squeezed out of a tube of oil paint. The rock was still a monochrome of white and grey tones, but it was now peppered with yellow and copper as the sun squeezed out color. The snow, white as paper, stopped shy of the lodge and extended frozen fingers of water from the summer thaw.

There was no discernable living thing in sight for what must have been a hundred kilometer crystalline view.

Terry roused himself up, standing quickly and mechanically, unfazed by the thin air. The polypropylene shirt clung to his bones. He came to my side, said "sun," and tottered out the door.

After breakfast we staged a paradigmatic group photo in front of the lodge, everyone passing their cameras back and forth like a family of Japanese tourists. As we prepared for the descent, Terry suddenly extended his arm and followed a military jet screaming over us at low altitude as it tracked into the valley below. The rest of us ducked.

"Man, he sure likes planes." Rick said.

Jill added eagerly, "That one went really fast didn't it, Terry? Do you like fast airplanes?"

Terry didn't answer. He followed the jet until its rumble faded, then he lowered his arm and resumed his blank stare. He raised his carefully arranged back pack and waited his turn to bring up the rear of our new line.

"Swiss Air Defense," Yoyo said. "We have an air force base right down there." He nodded into barren mountains before taking the lead down the trail. After throwing me a stern glance, Jill and her tender feet went next, and the others followed. Rick and his one good leg hobbled in front of me, and I took the slot in front of Terry.

"Mirage." Terry said.

"What, the base?" I replied.

"Mirage, III RS. French built. Flies fast and low. Good recon, but no good in a dog fight."

"You sure know your planes."

"I study them."

"What kind of school do you go to, Terry?"

"Embry-Riddle. Aerospace engineering. Got a grant from Boeing for this fall. Working on a new wing design."

Rick didn't flinch, evidently too absorbed in his game-plan, and Jill was too far ahead to hear the conversation. "Terry!" she called back. "Maybe we'll see some more really fast airplanes before we get down."

Descent is said by many to be hardest. Instead of pressing one's body purposely upward, gravity was there to help, and perhaps helping too much. Every step jammed my hip, knee, and ankle joints to where I felt bone on bone, and it was an act of restraint to keep from tumbling down the mountain. Yoyo was keenly aware and gave a knowing nod when he spotted the snowbank on the northeast slope. We were marching together like lemmings, adjacent to a minor spine, when Yoyo turned and stepped into the snowbank. He poked about with his alpenstock and picked up a handful of snow.

"A little icy, but this should be no problem. I'll go ahead first and signal you when I reach bottom."

Yoyo sat on his fanny, gave a kick, and off he went, picking up speed before turning into a dot. There was no tracking left or right, no swooshing or elegance involved, just a beeline to where the snow faded to stone. He slid to a stop and waved his arms.

"Everyone be quiet a minute. Listen," Rick said, having anointed himself leader in Yoyo's absence. We all stood in silence with our ears turned to the speck of a man waving his arms five hundred meters below. "Go. He said, 'Go! It's nice!' Cool. This is going to be great." Rick was happy to save his knee the wear. He sat first, adjusted his pack, and pushed off. "Going down!" He slid away until he also turned into a speck of a man. One by one, we all lined up with jittery excitement and stupid smiles on our faces. All except Terry. He crouched on one knee near the trail and fingered the snow, his head cocked sideways down the mountain.

"You go next," Jill said. "I'm tired of you lurking behind me."

Readying myself for launch, I tightened the straps on my day-pack and pulled my outer windbreaker over my butt for a slick ride. The first third of the descent was a calm amusement park ride. The mid-section was cause for some concern. The last leg was the fresh face of disaster. As the altitude decreased, the freeze-thaw action increased, and the snow field turned into an ice field. I accelerated through bumps and jags, and it felt like my clothes were burning away. I shifted from one cheek to the other to distribute the bruising, but I bounced onto my right side, digging an elbow into the ice and ripping off three layers of clothing and one layer of skin from elbow to shoulder. In an instant, I bounced onto my back where my telephoto lens jammed into a kidney. Righting myself back onto my ass coincided with the final approach where the snow was melting out and the rocks began to expose themselves. The first stone, a rather jagged loner, ripped open the side seam of my pants and spun me clockwise. The second was a direct hit, which I surprisingly glided right over. The third rock turned me into a tumbling bag of bones.

After sliding pathetically to a stop, I lay there gazing into the oil paint blue I had forgotten the name of. There were voices around me, all mumbling something or other. The only thing I could make out was Yoyo screaming, "No! . . . No! . . . It's ice!"

I sat up in time to see Jill's slide shriek to its conclusion about five meters away. She lost her backpack, her camera, and that silly Swiss climbing hat. Her eyes were wide and a strand of stringy hair wrapped around her nose.

I sat there in a stupor and checked for breaks among the bruises, but it was all cosmetic. My right tricep was congealing into a crusty red scab, and what remained of my right sleeve made a nice hand warmer. The others fared about the same. Rick lay there cussing, holding his bad knee with two bleeding arms. He had used his palms as brakes, leaving the skin of his forearms on the mountain. Although there were no Englishmen among us, it could be said that we were a bloody mess.

One by one, the members of our party climbed back up the snowbank, now a debris field, to retrieve broken cameras, lost clothing, and power bars. As I stood there holding my pants together, Terry stepped heedfully down the trail.

"Guys okay? Snow seemed a little icy."

Jill said nothing. She sat in the snow pulling fists of grated ice from under her parka. She looked as though her presence on the mountain was a simple misunderstanding.

Rick stood and balanced on one leg. He glared at Terry, then at me, and shook his head. "He didn't even have the guts to do it."

I glanced at the frail man on the edge of the trail and gave him a nod. Terry stood erect and intact. He looked past our folly, into the sun-filled valley with his usual blank stare, now punctuated by the slightest hint of a smile.

With These Hands We Inter

THE DRIVER OF THE CAR was crying for mercy, covering his face screaming, "*Au secours!*" as the windshield caved into his lap.

"Get off! Get away from him!" Adam yelled, elbowing his way through the mob. He held his bandaged hand close to his chest as people threw punches and grabbed his clothing, trying to pull him down. A dark-eyed man with a turtle-neck pulled over his face swung a piece of lumber at him, skimming his left ear. Adam leaned into him hard and they fell to the ground as the car was rolled over. A short-lived cheer rose from the street, drowning the driver's cries, but the crowd scattered when the police rushed in with batons drawn. Adam took several kicks to the back before he felt himself being pulled away by the collar. His good hand and forearm grated against the pavement and broken glass.

Self-preservation now trumped Adam's concern for the driver, or even his girlfriend, Sandrine, who he'd abandoned at the fringe of the storm. It didn't matter whose side anyone was on. French riot police were everywhere, taking prisoners of whomever they could catch. As Adam was being dragged away, he twisted his body and broke the officer's grip. He stumbled and was grabbed again, but then slipped from his coat and ran through a fresh cloud of tear gas and a hail of rocks. He grazed one of the steel bollards that lined the street and lunged for an iron fence to get his balance. Feeling his way along, he struggled to find a way out, a gap in the path or a sliver of light to pass through. Then the fence parted. Someone took him by the arm and pulled him from the riot. A few steps further and a heavy door closed behind him. He stood in sudden blackness, damp casket-like air, his eyes stinging badly and countless pains rising red over his body. The screams and taunts from outside were muffled and strangely far away.

"I saw what you have done," his guide said in French.

Adam caught his breath. "What happened to the driver?"

The man looked surprised when he heard Adam's accent. "He is being arrested. Better that than beaten to death." He was led to a straight back chair in the ambulatory of *Eglise Saint Severin*. "Wait here," he said. As the man's footsteps echoed away, Adam noticed his cloak. The man was a priest. He rubbed each eye with the ball of his palm. The lights in the ambulatory were not lit, making the rib vaulted ceiling cave-like, glowing dimly in red and blue from the stain glass windows. Adam's right hand and forearm were raw and bloody, and his left hand, already bandaged, was bleeding through the gauze. He felt his forehead and found a cut along the hairline. It wasn't until then that he wondered what had happened to Sandrine. She was just a little thing, and he hoped she wasn't foolish enough to have followed his charge into the fight.

The priest came back with a bowl of water and a tray of bandages, and began cleaning Adam's wounds with a damp sponge.

"Why are you here?" he asked.

Adam extended his bloody arm and tried to make a fist. "I'm a student," he said.

"You should have gone home until the protests are over. American?" he asked, and Adam nodded yes. "The streets now are not good for an American capitalist."

Having caught his breath and thinking less of the pain, he said, "I wasn't supposed to leave."

"Ahh. So you have some calling?" the priest said, smiling.

Adam winced as a sliver of glass was pulled from the back of his hand. "I promised someone I would stay."

The priest applied a bandage to his arm and another to his forehead. "I am afraid I have not done a good job. You can wait here until the crowd disperses, but then you must go to the hospital and get a proper dressing." Staring at his two wrapped hands, Adam nodded and thanked him. The priest carried his tray back to the sacristy.

Alone again in the forest of ancient columns of the double ambulatory, Adam rose and began wandering inside the church. He stepped onto the light bathed altar under the clerestories, but felt exposed and somehow vulnerable, so he crossed to the north side aisle where he came to a small chapel. The north windows lacked color and intensity, but added stillness to the space and enhanced the cold damp permanence of the stone walls and floor. To one side of the chapel was an altar supporting a simple glass case. Within, bound in red ribbon, were bones. The brass placard read, *Ex fociis sanctae Ursuloe.* Forever secured within were a piece of skull the size of a sea shell, a femur, and a little bundle of delicate bones tied like candy sticks. In the solemn chill of the space, Adam took in the modest shrine and felt something pass from him, as if something he had always relied on was now lost. He was tired and had no more fight in him. There was no more sound from the street, no more cries or threats, and it seemed at that moment, as Adam stood before the relics of the dead saint, that Paris had returned to its gracious self.

A rack for prayer candles on the opposite wall stood empty. Adam went to the small cabinet it sat on and opened a drawer. Inside were votives and a pack of matches. Using only the swollen pink tips of his fingers, he placed one of the votives in the rack and awkwardly struck a match. The flame spat and danced sporadically at first, as if uncertain it would carry on, but as a widening pool of wax formed beneath it the flame settled into a slim steady burn, one that might never extinguish.

∞

Three months before, Adam Legard had gone home to Washington, DC for Christmas and spent much of the time with his ailing mother as she waited for a bone marrow match that never came. He could see she was wearing down. Each day they went on walks together up and down New Hampshire Avenue, he helping her along by the arm, guiding her as she had always guided him. Monique Legard had aged twenty years in five, and her face was a landscape of fine determined lines. The long black hair she used to brush exactly one hundred times a day had fallen out and grown back twice over, but now she had given up on appearances, wearing a crochet cap only to keep her head warm.

"You look more like your father every day," Monique commented late one afternoon as the shadows were growing long. "And your father looked just like his father. We don't have a picture of your great grandfather, but I imagine he was the same."

Though she had told him this before, Adam took comfort in the resemblance as he longed for any connection to the father he had hardly known. The man's early death in a car accident left Adam with only vague remembrances from another age, his father's flesh frozen in time as the world passed on to other things. He often examined his face in the mirror, square-jawed with one long eyebrow, and tried to imagine the same face on another man at another time.

"If you get sick again, I'll come home right away," Adam said.

"No you won't," his mother objected. "You're not to interrupt your studies when my time comes."

Adam wanted nothing of this talk. He wanted her to fight. "When your time comes? You've beaten this before. You'll do it again."

"I want you in Paris when I die."

"No, mom."

"You'll heal from my death far easier away from the distractions of an American funeral. All those trite platitudes. What a mess." She spoke as if long ago convinced that most human rituals were mere folly. They turned down N Street where his mother liked to admire the few remaining brick row houses in the neighborhood. "Besides, I want you to find a nice French girl and fall in love."

"And what do I do in place of this mess of a funeral that I'm going to miss?"

Monique looked as if a butterfly landed on her wrist. "Stay in bed all day with your lover. Then go to one of the churches, maybe *Notre Dame* or *Saint Germain des Pres*," she said, perhaps thinking back to her husband and their own time there together. "Light a candle for me."

∞

When he first came to Paris in the fall, Adam walked each morning down *rue Monge* to the *quais* where he browsed the bookseller stalls for undiscovered treasures. His routine was a therapy of sorts, as he was lonely and slow to make friends until he was more confident with his French. But in the mid-winter, as the new labor law was passed and the protests began, the city transformed from intrigue to agitation. The streets were paved with a growing tension, and even the windows of buildings seemed to conceal a matrix of conspiracies. When Adam's sister, Ruth, called in early March with news of their mother's decline, Adam craved his old walks through the city, thinking they might revive his ill spirits, but the students, organized labor, and impoverished immigrants had taken over and turned the public face of Paris into a kind of riotous carnival. The student invasion even came to his building as neighbors opened their doors to kids from the suburbs and other cities. They stayed out until early in the morning and then were too hot and wired to sleep, frequently talking out their excitement until sunrise. Fifteen square meter studio flats were filled with five and six teenagers drinking wine, flushing toilets, and speaking of their utopian dreams. Between the political jabbering that passed through the wall and worried thoughts of his mother, Adam found little sleep.

In early March during the student occupation of the Sorbonne, despite the class strike and threatening slogans spray-painted in the hallways, Adam had tried to use one of the more remote classrooms to write a report on ancient burial rituals. When he left his papers and laptop for a moment to see if he could get into the library, a cadre of shouting students burst into the classroom and began throwing books, chairs, and fire extinguishers out the window at the police. Adam got back as the attack was subsiding and the students were advancing to a new front. He found his papers scattered on the floor. His laptop was gone. The sting of tear gas rose through the open windows and met his face as he squinted into the street where small fires were burning and reflecting off loose paving stones and shards of broken glass. Beyond a Maginot Line of entangled tables and chairs was a company of imperial looking riot police, helmeted, polished, awaiting orders. Sensing the final assault, he slipped downstairs and out through a barricaded side-street and made his way home. The Sorbonne fell that evening and had been closed ever since.

∞

Adam sat by the window in his studio flat and watched the latest wave of protesters descend *rue Monge* and flood the Latin Quarter. The unrest had moved into its second month, now organizing daily at *Place D'Italie* and invading the Left Bank in a multi-pronged assault. The French authorities had erected barricades around the Sorbonne, which only further emboldened the students who pounded their war drums, carried sagging banners, and raised signs that read *Retrait de CPE* and *Liberate le Sorbonne*! But the chants that rose from their angry mouths fell flat on Adam's ears as he gazed at them absently, feeling none of their rage. He was warming his hands on a cup of coffee when the front door rattled. Each of the three locks unlatched from top to bottom, and his girlfriend Sandrine came in wrapped in scarves.

"You said you would come," she said with her tender hip jutted to one side. "So come."

"I said I would think about it," Adam replied.

Sandrine had shaved her head on New Year's Eve and it was on that day that Adam walked into her bar on *rue Descartes* and watched her slender hands pour a pint of Guinness. Slight and wild, her personality bubbled like the caldron of beer she was drafting. Her bald head was perfectly shaped, like some river rock polished by the centuries. He had never seen anyone like her as she fluttered behind the bar and danced to Coldplay with the other bartenders. On hearing Adam's American accent, she stopped smiling, likely thinking him another tourist until he told her he was pursuing a masters in history at the Sorbonne.

Sandrine stepped across Adam's Spartan room. The flat was cold and furnished with only a single bed, a desk, and shelves loaded with history texts in French and English. In his time in Paris he had hung nothing on the walls. Sandrine raised a leg and straddled him. "You cannot sit here all day. It is pointless."

"And that's not pointless?" Adam said, gesturing outside.

Sandrine thumped him on the chest with her knuckles. "This is scandalous! Villepin has forced this law onto us. What you in America call railroaded. It is a railroaded law."

"A thirty-five hour work-week and six weeks of vacation aren't enough for you?"

"We are fighting for security. We have a right to work and a right for leisure." She got up and posed in front of the mirror. Adam took a breath and stared into the greying sky as she continued. "You call yourself an historian, yet you only sit by the phone all day and let history pass by."

"I call myself a lot of things, but not a rioter."

"There is no rioting."

Adam drew the curtain wider. Running single-file along the fringe of activists was a band of armed youths with their faces hidden under scarves and hooded sweatshirts. Earlier in the month they might have concealed their pipes and bats, but now they were emboldened and restless. "If this is a peaceful protest, then why are people covering their faces and carrying weapons?"

The struggle to be honest seemed to pain Sandrine. "The anarchists are more brazen. We fight for a cause, but they fight for no cause." She slouched and lost some of her exuberance. "They just fight."

"They burned a Gap store last week, and I heard they torched a McDonalds near Nation."

"That is not illegal," she said, rearranging her scarves.

Adam let the curtain fall. "Ruth should have called by now."

Sandrine came back to his side and knelt by him. She hadn't shaved her head for a week and a fine matt of hair began to define her face. Fully shaven, Sandrine possessed a kind of sensual anonymous appeal, but as Adam studied her he realized that with a full head of hair he might not recognize her. She took his hand and looked up to him.

"I am sorry about your mother, but you said she would not survive this time. And in a coma there is no pain." She squeezed his hand as he turned away. "It is still early in Washington. Your sister is probably asleep."

Adam grabbed the telephone, listened, and tapped the cradle.

"The line is out," he said. "Are they cutting the wires now?"

"See? Ruth cannot call you. Now will you please come with me?"

"Is that internet café open?"

"Everything is closed for the protests." Sandrine stood and took his hand. "Come. If you cannot ask for fair employment contracts, then perhaps you will find your computer lying in the street."

Adam could think of nothing to do. He had rarely left his flat since deserting the Sorbonne, going only to the local grocer and newsstand. Now cut off from home, which added a new spice to his worries, he felt restless and needed to walk. He put on his long coat and followed Sandrine down the five flights of spiraling stairs in his apartment block. The darkness of the narrow stairwell mixed with her earthy scent, and Adam felt the age of the city and the building and all those who had ever climbed those steps.

Though the sky was overcast, Adam squinted as they came onto the sidewalk in front of his flat. He followed Sandrine absently into the throng where *rue Monge* descended toward *Boulevard Saint Germain.* "I need something to drink," he said, taking her hand. On the far side of the street the small grocery where he shopped remained defiantly open. The shop-keepers had all been advised by the authorities to close their doors for the duration of the march, but under the threat of lost Euros a few rolled up their metal security gates and braved their country's youth. Inside the two aisle shop, Eva Roux, the elderly shop keeper, stood behind the counter looking troubled. On seeing Adam, she broke into a litany of complaints.

"I cannot run a business like this," she said. "Just yesterday a man with no face came in and stole drinks and boxes of biscuits and just ran away. The street full of people, police everywhere, and no witnesses."

"*Je regrette, Madame,*" Adam said, shaking his head. Sandrine grabbed two chilled bottles of water and went to the counter.

"These youth want guarantees in life," Eva Roux said.

"We want fairness, *Madame*." Sandrine dumped the plastic bottles by the register. "You know nothing of the CPE."

"That is not true. I might take on a clerk if I knew he would actually work. The last man I hired came in drunk every day and slept in the stockroom. I had to pay him for six months before I could legally terminate his employment."

"And now you can fire anyone for no reason at all!"

"Why would I do that? It is a capricious point of view."

"There is no security," Sandrine continued.

"And it is good to be paid for sleeping in my stockroom? Why must I support a drunk?"

Eva Roux's face was pained as Adam counted out the exact change. Sandrine was about to counter again when Adam grabbed her and said, "Let's go." He liked Madame Roux and wanted to be welcome there in the future.

As they got to the door, three hooded men plowed into Adam and sent him doubling back into his girlfriend. He and Sandrine fell against the shelves and crashed to the floor with the rattle of canned goods. Two of the men grabbed bottles of wine, and the third stuffed his pockets with Toblerone and other exotic bars of chocolate.

"*Arrêtez! Au voleur!*" Eva Roux cried out. "*J'appelle la police!*"

Adam jumped up and tried to grab the nearest intruder, but the man drew out a cast-iron pipe and swung wildly at the wine display, sending a blistering storm of glass and *vin rouge* into Adam's face.

"Filthy *casseurs!*" Sandrine screamed as the three thieves scurried out and disappeared into the masses. "You bring shame to our cause!"

The old lady rushed to the door and pulled down the security gate. Wine soaked into Adam's coat as little slivers of glass tinked to the floor. Blood dripped down his fingers and made a Jackson Pollack painting of scarlet red and deep burgundy on the linoleum. He raised his left hand and opened and closed the deep cut in his palm, then knelt and doubled over. Sandrine came to his side. She uncapped one of their bottles and poured water over the wound before squeezing the cut closed.

"You must apply pressure," she said, her voice shaking. Eva Roux hurried back with a roll of bandages and began wrapping Adam's hand.

"You must go to the hospital," she said.

"It's not that bad," he mumbled, fighting off the shock. "The wine will kill any infection."

"You are not funny," Sandrine said sharply.

"The clinic in the Sorbonne is closed."

"Then we will go to the hospital on *Île de la Cité*."

"Look at this mess!" Eva Roux exclaimed. "And they want jobs? Why would anyone hire them?"

"They are angry," Sandrine defended unconvincingly.

"Now I am angry too." She finished taping Adam's hand and stood. "You both must go. I cannot take any more of this today."

Adam got to his feet and examined his bandaged hand as they stepped to the door. "I am so sorry, Madame." He rolled up the gate just enough for he and Sandrine to slip under, leaving Eva Roux behind to sweep up the glass, blood, and wine.

Few of the peaceful demonstrators were willing to confront the riotous minority, preferring instead to carry banners and sing chants – CPE Equals Slave Contract and France is Ill. On *Boulevard Saint Germain*, where buildings were defiled with graffiti reading, Down with Work! and Let's Stop Being Reasonable, the protest moved as one giant organism, its cells pulsating together and multiplying amidst the trash, shattered ATMs, and husks of ruined kiosks. The throbbing in Adam's hand ran counter to the nerve grinding music of those banging and blowing on pocket-size instruments that together sounded like a high school marching band on some primitive aphrodisiac. A young woman with NON CPE smeared in red lipstick over her cheeks grabbed Adam's good hand and squeezed, as if supporting a wounded comrade. Now bumping shoulders in the crowd, Adam was surprised to see that most of the marchers, from young students to older workers, looked too happy to care about the senseless destruction around them. They seemed enthralled at being a part of something so large, a movement so collaborative and inclusive that the cause was secondary to the spirit of belonging.

At *rue Saint Jacques* a commotion was heard beyond a ruin of wrecked and overturned cars. Adam followed the sounds and spotted a masked hit squad ebbing and flowing up and down the street. Now after tasting an assault and acclimating to the wrongful pain in his hand, Adam felt strangely drawn to the violence.

He said to Sandrine, "I need to see this," and started up the hill.

"The hospital is the other way," Sandrine protested and ran after him. "Those people do not represent us!" They came within a block of the Sorbonne and watched the battle from behind an overturned car.

With each advance the radicals kicked the barricade in front of the university and threw cobblestones and bottles at the police, who in turn rushed them through an opening and nabbed the slowest agitators. As each was dragged away, a pack of cameramen dashed in for the prize winning photo before the pattern repeated itself.

"You say I'm witnessing history," Adam said, "but this is just a repeat. 1789, 1871, 1968 . . . last November."

"Do not belittle us," Sandrine objected.

"I'm not. Your history was made in the streets." He made eye contact with a man in filthy clothes and a ski-mask who had backed himself against a nearby building. He was breathing hard, eyes wild as he readied himself for the next assault. Adam saw in him a kind of timelessness, tinged with emptiness. The last time he felt that way was in the catacombs under the streets of Paris, staring into a different pair of expired eyes. "This is your tradition," he said, as the man sprang up and charged the barricade. The police unleashed a water cannon and hammered him to the pavement. Adam and Sandrine were close enough to feel the mist.

"May we go now?" Sandrine pleaded.

Adam relented and they turned back down *rue Saint Jacques*, toward *Île de la Cité*, and crossed the rising tide on the boulevard. The cars here too had been vandalized, but the street was now calm as groups of young men and women sat in circles on the glass strewn pavement eating lunch and playing instruments. Then one of the less damaged cars, a Peugeot sub-compact, unexpectedly lurched into the lane and began speeding around the clusters of students, who were diving from the car's path. People shouted obscenities at the driver and several banded together in front of the apse of *Eglise Saint Severin* to block his way. The driver looked scared and disoriented, unsure of which way to turn. The car stopped, but not before knocking down a female student and running over another's foot. From the multitude a mob quickly formed, and their curses turned into wielding fists as they began pounding the car and rocking it from side-to-side. The car's back window had already been shattered, and three hooded men pushed through and began smashing the other windows with sticks and clubs, trying to get to the driver.

"Idiot!" Sandrine exclaimed. The driver was paralyzed by fear, either unwilling or unable to fight for his own life. Adam was unwilling to stand by. He realized what was happening and rushed in. Mistaken at first as a brother-in-arms, the crowd seemed to open up and welcome him in, but as Adam pulled people away with his good hand and rammed them with his opposite shoulder, his conviction becoming apparent, the pack quickly turned and came down on him.

∞

The first thing Adam learned about Sandrine was that she was a *cataphile*. She had suspicious friends who had either keys to secret doors in the basements of the 5th and 6th Arrondissements, or who knew all the hidden access points in the far quarters of the city. For their second date, Sandrine had taken Adam to the last Metro stop on the #4 line south of the city, where along a sunken railroad they entered *les carrières de Paris*. This was the origin of the stone of the great churches of Paris. Mined from bedrock since Roman times, over three hundred kilometers of tunnels had served as the city's quarry, but was now a refuge for graffiti artists, heroin dealers and, to Adam's relief, amateur historians. But of all the littered and vandalized tunnels, chambers, and bunkers they covered, what left the greatest impression on Adam was the government sanctioned tour of the burial ossuaries from the late 18th century where the bones of seven million Parisians lie entwined in a kind of posthumous orgy. Twenty-five meters below the street were damp meandering passages defined by femurs stacked like cords of wood and patterned with hand polished skulls for symbol and scale. Each human wall made a burial pit where the lesser bones had been tossed in and melded together in a settled brush pile. Marble tablets memorialized the dead and indicated the extinct church from which they had been long ago exhumed. Here Adam was fascinated with life's circle of ironies: the bones of parishioners now filled the void where stone had been quarried to build their mighty churches. Here he witnessed the faceless masses from over two hundred years ago, stripped of flesh and identity, remembered as only a line in a history text or amusement for the curious.

Sandrine led Adam into the first avenue of the catacombs, raised her arms, and made a little pirouette. "I would like you to meet my great great grandparents."

"You can trace your ancestors here?"

"I don't see why not. These bones belong to all Parisians."

They meandered through the maze of human remains, in one chamber dodging drops of water that were calcifying the bones together as one. The last of the ossuaries was not filled from an overcrowded churchyard, but from rioting around the *Place de Greve* just before the French Revolution. Adam read the stone tablet.

"All these dead, just from riots," he said. Though the immigrant riots the prior Fall had not touched central Paris, the fires and violence from the evening news were still fresh in his mind. "Thousands of them," he said, as if trying to conjure up their faces.

"They died for a cause," Sandrine said with pride. Then she came up behind him and grabbed the soft flesh of his sides. "And now they are here with us." Backing him into a dark corner, she slid a hand down the back of his pants and kissed him. He returned the gesture and raised her shirt, kneading her bare back and running a hand over her polished head. With Sandrine's breasts pressed to his chest and the sharp knobs of femur bones kneeing him in the back, Adam glanced over her shoulder and saw, nestled deep within a cavity, the top half of a skull staring at them dispassionately.

A wave of sadness dampened Adam's arousal. How simply contained and arbitrary her once vibrant ancestors' bones had become. He wondered how the ones like Sandrine, ones so warm and alive and real in their own identity, could ever be so randomly tossed into the communal bone yard.

∞

By the end of April the CPE had been withdrawn and the protesters disbanded back into their old lives. Having won their battle for the status quo, the students regained their chaste and virtuous smiles, while the waiters and shopkeepers abided their time with their usual pained faces.

Adams's sister, Ruth, after arguing with airport security over having her mother's ashes probed for explosives, flew to Paris from Washington with the urn nestled between her feet. She and Adam ate lunch at a white-washed bistro in *Place de la Contrescarpe* and watched the young students gossip and flirt by the central fountain. The cafes were full of locals warming themselves in the spring sun. Adam and Ruth sat quietly, eating their *salade verte* and *tourte fromage*, yet they were very much a part of the vitality of the square. After their meal a gentle wind picked up. Adam ordered a café creme, and Ruth buttoned her sweater. As she took in the scene with jet-lagged eyes, Adam's gaze fell on his sister's profile. He stared intently at her fine expressive mouth and angular cheeks, and for the first time noticed that Ruth bore the imprint of their mother.

Ruth reached for her purse. "I wrote down some of the places where mom said she used to go with dad." She unfolded a piece of paper and read aloud the names of a Left

Bank theater and several boutiques. "Those antique shops she used to talk about were on *rue Jacob*." She slid the list across the table, but Adam didn't need it.

"They're still there," he said, examining the long red scar across his palm. "I'll take you this afternoon."

Up to that morning, Adam had mourned alone. Perhaps sensing his distance and wanting him to open up, Ruth bent her mouth into a mischievous smile only a sister could contrive. "Now tell me about this bald woman you were dating. How did that happen?"

Adam blushed and stirred his café creme. "I really don't know. She liked history." He watched as a grim-faced waiter came to the next table and began wiping it clean. "I guess she was what I needed at the time."

Bathed in the warm sun of spring, the pull of the square was great – a grounding force, a call to resist change as they were part of a living thing. It was the living consciousness of the place, taking part in the community flesh and blood that made Adam long for something of permanence.

After paying the bill, the siblings rose and carried their mother's remains down *rue Descartes*, past the bar where Adam's ex-lover danced to Coldplay, and past the battle ground of *rue des Ecoles*, where the air was full of the sound of city workers sand-blasting graffiti off Haussmann-era buildings. Closer to the Seine they veered onto a narrow medieval street where the noise subsided and Paris again felt enduring, though to Adam not without its silent scars. On the *quai de la Tournelle*, beneath unfurling buds of ancient sycamores, they met water, uncapped the urn, and watched quietly as the ages slipped through their fingers.